ANDY BRIGGS
HERO.COM

Chaos
Effect

OXFORD

UNIVERSITY PRESS

For everyone who convinced me it was possible!

OXFORD
UNIVERSITY PRESS

Great Clarendon Street, Oxford OX2 6DP

Oxford University Press is a department of the University of Oxford.
It furthers the University's objective of excellence in research, scholarship,
and education by publishing worldwide in

Oxford   New York

Auckland   Cape Town   Dar es Salaam   Hong Kong   Karachi
Kuala Lumpur   Madrid   Melbourne   Mexico City   Nairobi
New Delhi   Shanghai   Taipei   Toronto

With offices in

Argentina   Austria   Brazil   Chile   Czech Republic   France   Greece
Guatemala   Hungary   Italy   Japan   Poland   Portugal   Singapore
South Korea   Switzerland   Thailand   Turkey   Ukraine   Vietnam

Oxford is a registered trade mark of Oxford University Press
in the UK and in certain other countries

British Library Cataloguing in Publication Data

Data available

ISBN: 978-0-19-272969-9

1 3 5 7 9 10 8 6 4 2

Printed in Great Britain by CPI Cox & Wyman, Reading, Berkshire

Paper used in the production of this book is a natural,
recyclable product made from wood grown in sustainable forests.
The manufacturing process conforms to the environmental
regulations of the country of origin.

What a brilliant idea! One set of books,
featuring superheroes and one featuring
supervillains—and told through the eyes
of teenagers! Each series complete
in itself yet each referring to the other.
Original, imaginative and exciting!
Who could ask for anything more?
Excelsior!

Stan Lee

From: Andy Briggs
To: HERO.COM readers everywhere
Subject: Careful on the web!

As you know, the Internet is a brilliant invention, but you need to be careful when using it.

In this awesome book, the heroes (and villains!) stumble across the different websites accidentally. But HERO.COM and VILLAIN.NET don't really exist. :-(
I thought them up when I was dreaming about how cool shooting ice out of my mouth would be. The idea for HERO.COM suddenly came to me—especially the scene where Toby becomes digitized into a computer . . . Oh hang on! You haven't read it yet so I'd better shut up! :-) Anyway, I began writing and before I knew it, the idea had spiralled into VILLAIN.NET as well. But I had to make up all of the Internet stuff. None of it is really out there on the web.

Here are my tips for safe surfing on the web: keep your identity secret (like all good superheroes do), stick to safe websites, make sure a parent, teacher or guardian knows that you're online—and if anyone sends you anything that makes you feel uncomfortable, don't reply, and tell an adult you trust.

I do have my own website, and it's totally safe (even without superpowers!):
www.whichsideareyouon.co.uk

Be safe out there!

:-)

CONTENTS

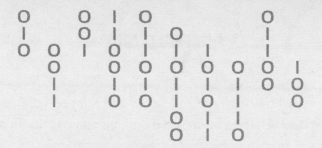

The Arrival

Lord Destructo was, in a word, unbeatable.

An expert on causing chaos, he swung the battleaxe with such devastating force that he swiped three enemies in half with a single swing, laughing evilly as he did so.

'You're goin' down!' goaded a painfully thin robed man with a crooked, pointy nose. A cone of light erupted from his palms.

Destructo was fast; in the blink of an eye he deflected the blast with a hexagonal shield. The energy ricocheted back on the thin man and he vanished in a puff of smoke.

'I am invincible!' roared Destructo. He was thoroughly enjoying himself. It had taken a long time to rise to such power, and he was determined to make the most of it. Another wave of warriors raced towards him, swords raised.

'Get him!'

'I'm gonna lob your head off, dude!'

'Nobody messes with me!' bellowed Destructo. He

dropped his battleaxe and shield and jumped agilely to his right. Despite his massive bulk he moved with fluid grace, emulating moves of seasoned free-runners.

Destructo bounced from a wall, pirouetted gracefully over his opponents' heads, then landed and dealt a flurry of martial arts blows that were almost impossible to follow.

Two of his opponents vaporized into nothing, the third was sprawled on the ground, his weapon cast aside.

'No way, man! Gimme a break!'

Destructo retrieved his battleaxe and advanced menacingly. 'Lord Destructo gives no mercy!'

'Trevor!' The voice came out of nowhere. It threw Lord Destructo off his murderous rampage. For a moment he thought his secret name had been uttered and looked around for the culprit.

'Trevor!'

It was enough of a distraction for the guy on the floor to roll to his sword and stab it into Destructo's gut. The villain recoiled, dropping his axe.

'He shoots! He scores!' hollered the swordsman jubilantly. He raised the blade for another blow.

Destructo's hands suddenly glowed bright red—a shimmering heat-ray disintegrated the swordsman. For a second, there was nothing left but a charred skeleton holding a sword, then it vanished.

'Trevor! Your dinner's going cold!'

The Arrival

Lord Destructo froze as the console game was paused. Trevor Jones irritably threw the controller down. He yanked off his headset and glared at his closed bedroom door.

'In a minute! You nearly got me killed!' he bellowed at the top of his lungs. His mum's timing was typically bad. Why was it parents always knew the moment you were having the most fun, just so they could interrupt it?

'Now, Trevor! I won't tell you again!'

'Good! I'm not hungry anyway!' he muttered under his breath.

He looked at his alter ego on the screen. It represented months of playing online and missed homework. It was a work of art, but his mum wouldn't appreciate that; apparently eating with the family was much more important. Now he would surely die if his character didn't find a safe refuge.

Trevor sighed and picked the controller up to save his game play. Out of the corner of his eye, the character seemed to move. It was a subtle thing and impossible because the game was still paused.

He squinted at the screen . . . but nothing happened. His thumb hovered over the game pad, a click away from saving the game and giving up. Then he caught the movement again in his peripheral vision.

This time the movement continued when he stared

directly at it. The graphics were distorting, each pixel shimmering. Trevor was concerned; now was not the time for the game to crash. His thumbs danced across the controller—no response.

'Don't do this to me!' He punched every button on the pad, just in case it magically restored the game. 'Great!' he spat at the screen. Resetting the console would erase the entire day's worth of play. Weighed down with reluctance, he reached for the power button—

And the screen suddenly exploded! The television itself remained intact, but the room was filled with swirling pixels as though a swarm of miniature bees had entered the room.

Trevor swatted at them as they rolled across him. It was like being inside a sandstorm. He felt sharp tingles of electricity as pixels struck him in their thousands, forcing him to his knees.

A loud CLUMP made the floor shake.

Through tear-filled eyes, Trevor watched in horror as something stepped out of the screen—something huge and muscular and alarmingly familiar.

It was Lord Destructo!

Trevor gasped in shock—a bad move as his mouth was suddenly filled with pixels, popping in his mouth like space candy and stifling his scream.

He fell on his back, scrambling away on all-fours

The Arrival

as Destructo pulled himself to his full height. Even through the swarm, Trevor could see the creature was not quite real. His features were angular, made from thousands of polygons, just like in the game. The textures on his body seemed flat and unconvincing when set against his bedroom. Trevor backed against his wardrobe—he could go no further.

Destructo flexed his arms, staring at them as if for the first time. He looked satisfied. Then he raised both fists to the ceiling and roared. The sound was a cross between a foghorn and an electronic warble.

'Trevor! I told you to turn that off!' came the distant voice of his mum from downstairs. Trevor tried to call for help, but his mouth was full of solid pixels. 'Now get down here, or you'll be in trouble!'

Destructo's gaze suddenly fell on the cowering boy. It was difficult to gauge a reaction on the polygon face, but Trevor thought it must be delight. The digital avatar leant forward and easily picked him up by the scruff of his shirt.

The monster spoke . . . or tried to. What came out was a garbled distortion that cycled through pitch and frequency until the sounds started to emulate words that sounded like a bad radio transmission.

'It has worked! I am free! Finally!'

Trevor lashed out. His knee clanged into the fiend's very solid private parts, a strike that would have felled anyone else. Then Trevor had a stroke of luck. His shirt ripped at the seams and he dropped to the floor. For once, he was thankful he was overweight! He scrambled for his bedroom door and managed to open it—before the swarm of pixels slammed it shut, almost trapping his fingers.

Destructo lunged forward and grabbed Trevor firmly around the neck, lifting the boy off his feet. The avatar's mouth hyperextended, like a snake's jaws, and Trevor caught sight of the dark tunnel beyond, stretching impossibly far. Electricity crackled in the yawning cyber-gullet.

It was the last thing he saw before he was consumed whole by the digital abnormality.

'Right!' screamed his mother from behind the closed door. 'I've had enough! I'm banning you from wasting your time on that computer!'

She swung the door open and looked around the empty room. The place was a mess, as if a hurricane had torn through it. That was normal. What was unusual was the fact that Trevor was missing. She had heard noises from the room seconds earlier, and the windows were all closed.

She peeked in the wardrobe, just in case he was hiding there. She didn't notice the console turning itself off; the green power light turned hostile red.

Cadet Training

Toby Wilkinson's concentration was starting to drift as he looked across the rooftop to the skyscraper opposite. He was standing fifty metres above the city and the biting cold wind was so relentless miniature icicles were forming on his runny nose. He had once been stranded in Antarctica, but somehow Toronto felt much colder. He sighed as his mind wandered.

Working with a team required trust between teammates, but he wasn't feeling very inspired with his choice of companions. He was used to saving the day with his sister, Lorna, and their friends Pete and Emily, but that had all gone wrong and friendships had been torn apart. Pete had drifted to the Council of Evil then found his way to lead a new group of rogues called Forge, created by Mr Grimm—a back-stabbing 'hero' Toby had once trusted.

Forge was originally created as the more neutral choice between the Foundation and the Council, but in truth their activities were just as self-serving and they appeared to vacillate between the two extremes in an anarchic fashion. That was probably down to Pete; he had never possessed great leadership skills.

Toby's sister, Lorna, had dated Jake Hunter who was their school's toughest bully and one of the world's most lethal supervillains. To be fair, she hadn't known he was a villain at the time. But now she did know, she still seemed to like the creep and Toby couldn't figure out why. She was starting to turn into one of those freaky girls who wrote to serial killers on death row.

To top it all off, Emily, whom Toby had started to quite like, had begun pining for Pete and had gone on a mission to guide him away from the self-destructive path he had embarked upon.

Who said life was simple?

Eric Kirby, the head of the Foundation, had promised Toby that once the new cadets were trained, then the Foundation would gather its forces and attack the Council of Evil headquarters. Toby was one of the few superheroes that had been to the mysterious island complex and survived. He escaped with valuable details of the Council's top-secret location.

Toby had unexpectedly found himself promoted as one of the Foundation's most trusted assets, and as such he was starting to be too valuable to use in dangerous situations. That meant he was now forced to train the newbies. The only perk of the job was that he was working with Jen, a rather attractive sixteen-year-old

Cadet Training

Japanese American, whom he had met when they were fighting one another. She looked more mature, easily passing for eighteen, and she was yet another complication in his chaotic life.

'See anything new, shrimp?' asked Jen over his headset.

Toby was brought back to the situation in Toronto. As much as he liked Jen, he hated her nickname for him. He was sure she did it to wind him up. Toby squinted and felt a rush of dizziness as his vision zoomed in on the windows of the tower across the street.

'Nothing's changed. The hostages are still in place.'

Twenty hostages were pressed against the windows on the penultimate floor of the skyscraper. They were leaning forwards with all their weight on their hands. The idea was that if somebody tried to come in through the window then the hostages would fall as the glass broke. Toby had to admit it was an effective solution. Nothing had changed for the last three hours and that was worrying Toby because he had no idea how long his three downloaded powers would last.

He'd selected them from the Hero.com website at home before leaving. The Foundation had given him a cool touchscreen mobile phone that had several raw powers preloaded in tiny cylinders built into the body, teleportation being the one he used to get to the crisis scene.

He had pleaded with Kirby to have access to more than three powers, but the bar was firmly set after everybody witnessed the mutating effects over-consumption had on Pete.

Toby shivered, that had been a bad day. They had been on the Foundation's floating headquarters when a supervillain called Basilisk had attacked. Pete had bravely tackled the fiend, but the resulting fight saw Pete hurled through multiple vats of raw superpowers. Nobody had ever absorbed so many different powers in such vast quantities and it had imbued him with the gift to combine powers into new ones. The side affect was that his body and mind had been twisted. That's when Toby truly lost his best friend.

The unreliable duration of the powers was another factor Kirby refused to address for the same reasons—a longer duration would require a greater dosage. The only way round it was by downloading 'one use' powers from the Bluetooth headset cupped against his ear. That was voice controlled, and one of the Foundation's cooler new inventions.

Another factor bothering Toby was that he was supposed to get back home to attend a family party. He knew Lorna would cover for him if he was late, but if he didn't show then he would be in trouble. His parents had already hinted at confiscating his computer if he didn't buck his ideas up.

Cadet Training

'We've got to get in there and do something,' said Toby restlessly.

'You heard what the boss said. We observe and wait,' replied Jen over the headset.

The 'boss', in this case, was a superhero called Chameleon. He was a Prime, somebody born with latent superpowers rather than a Downloader like Toby. Chameleon wanted the authorities to handle the situation because the gunmen didn't appear to be wielding any superpowers. Toby's team was only on standby in case anything went wrong. The world had had too many close calls recently due to warring heroes and villains and it was becoming a strain to keep the existence of superpowers from the Press, and each event made it more difficult. Chameleon felt that if the authorities could cope, then so much the better.

Toby shivered as he scanned the windows. He stopped and backtracked as he noticed movement behind the hostages. Several masked men were unrolling coils of coloured wires. Toby watched as the gunmen strung the wires to blocks of putty-like C4 plastic explosive and attached them to the walls behind the hostages.

'Uh, Jen? We've got a big problem.'

'You need to go to the toilet again?' she fired back.

'No. This is a little more serious . . . although I really needed to go then. I was bursting,' he added defensively. Even superheroes had to answer the call of nature.

'You're rambling, shrimp.'

That was the problem with talking to Jen, he liked the sound of her voice. She was a distraction he didn't need right now.

'The hostage takers are wiring the floor with explosives.'

'That's so not good,' replied Jen, the master of understatement.

Toby switched his gaze to the streets below. The police had cordoned off the area, although a huge crowd of media and thrill-hungry spectators watched from behind barriers.

Vans had started to arrive carrying more cops. Toby had been hoping to see some of the bright red jackets of the Royal Canadian Mounted Police, but was disappointed to see they looked just like ordinary officers.

Some heavily armed SWAT-like guys had pulled up in a van and slowly advanced on the front entrance.

'ETF has joined the party,' commented Jen. Toby had been told to expect them. The Emergency Task Force was a team of tactically trained police officers who specialized in exactly these types of circumstances. Toby had hoped they would turn up earlier, now it was looking a little too late.

Cadet Training

'They have no idea what they're running into. Maybe it's time to deploy Dumb and Dumber?'

Jen chuckled. 'You're terrible. They're lovely guys.'

Toby was referring to the two new Downloaders they were charged with training. Chameleon had told him they were the best, but if that was the case, then there was no hope for the Foundation.

'Well?' prompted Toby. He looked across to the building on the opposite side of the hostage situation where he knew Jen was watching. He couldn't see her though.

Below, the ETF had forced their way into the lobby. That single action had violated the hostage takers' list of demands. The elevators were out, so the ETF would be forced to make their way laboriously up the staircase.

'Jen? Can you hear me?'

'I'm thinking,' she snapped back. She always got tetchy with him under pressure. 'I don't see that we have any choice.'

'Well . . . we could always go in instead.'

'Right, and what have you downloaded that would help?'

Toby didn't reply: she was right. They had both selected powers suited to observing the situation. Neither possessed any combat powers to take the gunmen out. If things went badly, then they could only hope that Chameleon turned up with reinforcements; but he wasn't even in the same country.

'Toby, send them in.'

Toby grunted in reply and pulled out his mobile phone. He hit a button to initiate a video chat. Almost twenty seconds passed before a cheerful face appeared with a slice of pizza halfway to his mouth.

'Yo!'

Toby inwardly groaned. Dumber had answered the phone.

'Hayden? What took you so long answering? You're supposed to be on stand by!'

'I had to pay the pizza guy, man. Chill!' Hayden's surf-boy looks perfectly matched his voice.

Toby wished he could punch the screen so his fist would come out on the other end of the line and chin Hayden.

'We need you and Moron Two to get in there and rescue the hostages.'

Hayden grinned his dazzling smile. 'Far out!'

'Be warned, there is a police team in the building and the gunmen have planted explosives . . . ' Toby drifted off as he was talking to an anchovy. Hayden had thrown his pizza close to his camera and run out, not even bothering to terminate the call.

Toby glanced at his watch. If they could resolve things in the next fifteen minutes he could still make it home without getting into trouble.

Somehow he doubted it would be that easy.

Cadet Training

* * *

Arid Larkin was a small-time crook with big plans. This was the most daring job he had ever taken on, and he was pleased it was going so smoothly. Their employer had planned every aspect of the raid with minute precision, and it had paid off. There had been no casualties, the police had behaved exactly as expected and they had broken into the vault on the fiftieth floor with relative ease. Now their satchels had been emptied of their explosives and filled with plans and prototypes of a new generation of computer processor that would see all twelve men rich beyond their wildest dreams once they had delivered them to their employer. All they had to do was get them out.

A silent alarm flashed on the netbook computer sitting on one gunman's lap. It was linked to sensors they had placed across their building to detect forced entry. The men were too well trained to have to speak. A series of complex hand signals told his companions that fifteen armed police had stormed the lobby and were ascending on the north staircase.

Larkin glanced through the window searching for the helicopter he knew was coming. They had issued lengthy ransom demands to the police; not that he cared about results, it was only a stalling tactic. When their own helicopter arrived they would blow up the top floor—hostages and all. That would keep the emergency services busy.

Then he saw the fast-moving chopper approaching them. He turned and signalled to his men to get ready. When he looked back the helicopter had vanished.

He squinted, certain he had seen it. He pulled the heavy facemask off; the hostages were all pressed against the window so they wouldn't see his face. Even if they did, they would be blown into very small chunks soon.

He shielded his eyes against the sun and stared through the window. He spotted the helicopter again— but there was something seriously wrong. The aircraft was rushing towards him—rotor first, as if thrown by a mighty hand.

A gust of wind suddenly blew through the office block—and the hostages vanished from their positions against the windows.

'What is going on?' he bellowed.

His companions looked round in shock—they had all seen their hostages vanish in front of their eyes. They stared out of the window as—

The helicopter smashed through the floor-to-ceiling windows. Gnashing rotor blades tore up the floor, ceiling, and any furniture in the way.

Larkin ran for his life as the wall of swirling rotor blades advanced metres behind him. He threw himself over a bank of metal filing cabinets, just in time, as the C4 explosives, caught in the blades, detonated.

Toby watched from the rooftop opposite, his mouth slack as the entire top corner section of the building erupted in a massive fireball. The explosives had been wired together, but the whirling rotor had reeled them all in, resulting in the focused blast and ensuing mass devastation.

The hostages had been whisked to 'safety'. In this case they were all on the rooftop and screaming as the building shook around them and flames punched up from the corner office.

Toby's gaze switched to Hayden who was hovering several hundred metres away. The grin had slipped from the cadet's face. He was the one who had intercepted the chopper and thought it would be an awesome idea to throw it at the bad guys.

Larkin poked his head up from behind the dented filing cabinets. The floor ended centimetres away and the corner of the building was missing as though some giant monster had bitten it off. Jagged metal girders hung limply out of the floor and walls. The explosion had taken out the floor above, but not the roof above that—which was the very top of the building where the hostages stood. Everything seemed on fire, and the suspended quarter creaked as it wobbled over the drop, fuelling the screams of the hostages above.

Larkin had no idea what had gone wrong, and he didn't want to wait to find out. He careered further into the building; he knew he had to find another means of escape.

A blond boy suddenly landed in the hallway blocking his path. Larkin looked frantically around, the kid must have jumped down from the floor above, that was the only explanation. What troubled him was the fact that the boy wasn't more than sixteen and he was smiling.

'Man, that was, like, impressive! But we've got your number now, dude. You're under arrest.'

Larkin went for the pistol in his thigh holster—but it wasn't there. It must have fallen out when the helicopter crashed. He doubled-back. There was something about the boy that made him not want to start a fight. It was the way he was grinning inanely. Larkin bumped into two of his men as they raced down the corridor. He didn't care where the others had gone, they were only hired muscle.

They rounded another corner—and the boy was standing there, blocking his path! Impossible!

'*Guten Tag!*' said the smiling boy. Larkin hesitated— it was impossible that he had overtaken them, and his accent was distinctively German. 'The hostages are safe and you are going nowhere, *ja?*'

'Get him!' Larkin screamed at his two companions. They went for their firearms. The kid swept both his hands apart and the two men were plucked off their feet and thrown through the thin corridor walls—crashing into the offices beyond.

'That's impossible!' screamed Larkin in terror. He turned and fled the way he had come.

He hurtled back into the partially demolished office and was brought up short by the sight of his team bound together with the detonation cord they had primed the explosives with. The kid was there, tying the knot. He looked up nonchalantly.

'Hey. You giving up already?'

'How do you do that?' demanded Larkin. He was looking around for any weapon he could use.

'Do what?'

Larkin's eyes fell on an explosive satchel that miraculously hadn't detonated. He ran for it, sliding along the paper-strewn floor to scoop it up. He jammed a detonator into the explosive and held it aloft.

'Touch me and we all blow up!' he yelled.

'Man, you're crazy, you'll die too.'

'It's better than going to jail!'

Larkin suddenly noticed the boy's double run into the office. He stopped, assessing the scene.

'Two of you? How can there be two of you?'

'Jurgen's my identical twin, bro.'

For a second, the bizarreness of the situation was overriding the danger. 'But you don't sound the same.'

Jurgen snorted a laugh. 'Duh! Identical in looks. Father took Hayden to America, I lived in Germany with mother,' he explained in his thick Germanic accent.

'Easier to tell us apart,' laughed Hayden. Neither seemed fazed by the bomb. 'Now why don't you give in, man? The hostages are safe on the roof,' a chorus of screams from the rooftop didn't seem to worry him, 'thanks to Jurgen's super-bad speed, and the rest of your buddies ain't going nowhere.'

Larkin hesitated. It suddenly made sense why his employer hadn't attempted the theft himself when Larkin was faced with an army of supermen. He lowered the explosive satchel.

Hayden nodded. 'Cool. You're a smart dude after all.' He unhooked a phone from his belt and thumbed a digit. 'Yo, Tobe, Jen. Bad guys are nabbed, good guys are saved.'

'Who are you?' asked Larkin, completely out of his depth.

'Ain't it obvious?' Hayden extended his arms like a showman, he was enjoying every moment of showing off. 'We're superheroes, dude.'

Toby and Jen flew in through the gouge in the corner of the ceiling. Larkin's mouth fell open in shock.

'You can fly?'

Toby ignored him, instead he rounded on the twins, pointing at the destruction. 'Look what you did!'

Cadet Training

Jurgen's bottom lip stuck out defiantly. 'We finished the mission, did we not?'

'Have you ever heard of "collateral damage"?' shrieked Toby.

'Go easy on them, Tobe,' said Jen in a measured voice. 'I'm sure your first time in the field wasn't plain sailing?'

Toby bit his lip. His first time was a story he didn't want to get into right now.

Larkin held up his hand, he felt as if he was suddenly back at school. 'Excuse me?'

Nobody was listening.

'Don't side with them, Jen,' groaned Toby. 'You can't seriously expect this to be classed as a successful mission?'

'Excuse me?'

Jen brushed her long jet-black hair over one shoulder and crossed her arms, a sure sign the conversation was over.

'Yes I do. The hostages are all safe, these bozos have been stopped.'

'EXCUSE ME!' bellowed Larkin. Now everybody looked at him. He raised the explosive satchel high. 'Now I have your attention, maybe you'll want to listen to me. This ain't over.'

'I'm pretty sure it is, bro,' said Hayden flippantly.

'Shut up!' Toby hissed at him. Then he turned to

Larkin and spoke in a much calmer voice. 'It is over. Put the explosives down.'

Larkin laughed. Some of his arrogance was returning. His employer had prepared a back-up plan; Larkin had thought there would be no need to implement it.

He edged over to his tied-up men. The heroes gave him a wide berth. They had several powers between them, but none of them had the power to survive an explosion.

'You're not going anywhere,' said Jen defiantly.

Larkin reached his men, but rather than try to undo the knot, he picked up a bulky backpack and slipped it on.

'I think you'll find that I am leaving you. Blondie put the hostages on the roof.' He nodded at Jurgen and smiled evilly. 'Excellent.'

Then he threw the satchel across the office, towards the ceiling. The four heroes instinctively tracked the satchel as Larkin charged for the edge of the building and leapt outside.

Hayden shoved Jen out of his line of sight and craned his neck forward.

'NO!' screamed Toby.

But it was too late. Fine laser beams shot from Hayden's eyes and detonated the satchel. Toby only had time to tackle Jen to the floor as the C4 explosives inside exploded, taking out a massive chunk of the ceiling overhead.

The corner of the roof groaned as support beams were obliterated and dropped down into their office, forming a forty-five-degree slide off the skyscraper.

The office was choked with smoke and dust. Toby could just see the hostages sliding down the inclined roof and plummeting to their doom.

Toby and Jen acted as one. They aimed for a smashed section of wall and jumped out. They took flight and in a split-second had assessed what was happening.

The majority of the hostages were still on the roof. Eight had been standing on the slab of roof that angled down and they had slid off the edge. Six dangled from steel supports poking from the concrete while two fell like stones.

Jen and Toby dived for the falling hostages. Toby noticed Larkin out of the corner of his eye—the criminal's backpack opened and a compact parachute blossomed out.

Toby couldn't spare the time to pursue him. He zeroed in on a falling woman and grabbed hold of her. Her wild screams suddenly stopped as she stared at Toby, who was covered in dirty dust and debris as if he had been used to sweep a chimney.

'I've got you!' he said in the most reassuring voice he could in the circumstances.

'Yeah . . . but who has got *you?*' squeaked the girl.

It was a fair point. Toby's flight powers were not strong enough to support the two of them and stop her from falling, but he could at least slow her descent. He aimed for the top of an ambulance; it was the most appropriate landing pad he could think of.

They crunched down on the roof, buckling the metal. Toby noticed Jen had made a more elegant landing on a patch of grass. Toby shot back into the sky before the saved girl could thank him.

Jen joined him racing back to the dangling figures on top of the tower—just as one lost his grip and plummeted past.

'Mine!' yelled Jen and suddenly peeled away to save the guy.

Toby managed to drag the five hanging office workers back up the inclined section of roof, and to safety. Jurgen, Hayden, and Jen joined him as he pulled the last woman up.

Toby was boiling with anger. He stabbed a finger at the twins, who had the good sense to look abashed.

'You idiots! What happened to stealth? What happened to playing it cool and using minimum force?'

'We used hardly any powers to attack them.'

Toby gaped, looking between the ragged missing corner of the building and the twins.

Cadet Training

'No force?' Toby spluttered indignantly. 'Hayden, you chucked a helicopter through a window!'

'Tobe, you were awesome,' said Jen with wide appreciative eyes. The effect of her smile immediately threw Toby off his rant.

Hayden nodded. 'She's right, man, that was quick thinkin'. I hope we're like you someday.'

Toby listened for a hint of sarcasm, but there was none. Then his phone beeped for attention—he had to leave to make it to the family party.

'Fine. You guys can sort out this mess. I have to go.' He hit the teleporter on his phone and vanished in a clap of thunder.

The twins looked at Jen, who simply held up her finger to silence them.

'Don't say a word. Let's just get out of here and we can discuss how we could've approached this situation a little more delicately.'

The bewildered hostages watched as their three arguing saviours instantly vanished with a bang. They couldn't fathom what had just happened to them.

The Message

Eric Kirby sighed as he watched the footage on the video monitor for the fifth time. Each time it never got better. He tapped a key on the control panel and the screen went blank.

He leant back in his chair, one hand absently stroking a crystal-like pendant that hung around his neck.

'What have I done?' he whispered to himself. For decades he had striven to create the HERO Foundation to protect the world and give others the chance to exploit wonderful gifts normally reserved for the chosen few.

Hero.com had been the backbone of the Foundation's success and had propelled the organization into the digital age. But, like all corporations, the Foundation had grown greedy. It had started innocently enough when Hero.com started charging for downloading its powers in a mistaken attempt to encourage heroism. 'Heroic Points' were given as credit for genuine actions; without them you had to pay for the powers. Once the money had starting coming in, the

Foundation looked for other ways to cover running expenses.

Kirby mused that that was the beginning of the Foundation's slow decline. The cracks were not visible on the surface, but they were amongst those who ran the show. Petty jealousies and arguments were becoming commonplace and interfering with their work. He thumbed a communications button.

'Chameleon?'

A tired voice came over the intercom. 'I'm here.'

'I've reviewed the security footage.'

'And?'

'Have you seen it?'

'I haven't had a chance. How bad can it be?'

The question was left hanging for several seconds. Kirby had the sudden urge to admit he had pushed things too far and it was his own fault, but that wouldn't help the situation. The proverbial cat was out of the virtual bag. 'And we need to talk.'

He cut the communication. He couldn't bear one of Chameleon's glib one-liners that seemed to flow from his mouth with increasing regularity. The hero was changing, becoming more cynical and more concerned with capturing the Dark Hunter. Kirby was starting to feel the pressure . . . and his age.

He knew there wasn't much time left for him, the Foundation . . . and possibly the world.

The Message

* * *

'What on earth happened to you?' screeched Toby's mum the very second she laid eyes on him as he entered the function room.

After the disaster zone in Toronto, Toby had been thinking about getting to the party on time. Teleportation relied on the user to think of their destination. He should have visualized home instead so he could get a shower and a quick change of clothes; the ones he wore now were stained black and smelt as if he'd been in a fire.

Toby looked guiltily around the packed function room. Everybody was giving him funny looks, but he was beyond caring. He had been forced to attend this wedding reception. He normally endured family functions with good grace, but this was some remote cousin's wedding and half the faces peering at him were unfamiliar.

'There was an accident, a fire, and I just got caught downwind of it,' he improvised. Toby hadn't been a good liar, but working with the Hero Foundation had, oddly, made him a much better one. 'Maybe you or Dad can drive me home to get changed?' he added hopefully.

'Not a chance. I've had a couple of glasses of wine, and your father . . . ' She glanced at the bar where her husband was in full swing recounting his new miraculous find in Cambodia: a lost city that, unbeknownst to him, his son had found and subtly laid the clues for the official discovery.

After cleaning himself up as best he could in the shabby toilets, Toby contented himself with a welcome cold drink and sat in the corner, away from the searching eyes of vague relatives. He put his mobile phone on the table and hoped it wouldn't flash indicating a Foundation emergency. Now he knew how hospital doctors felt being on call all the time—and this was supposed to be the relaxing half term! His sister, Lorna, found him quickly enough.

'Where have you been?' she asked rather sharply.

'Oh, you know, surfing the net.' That was their code for downloading powers from Hero.com and flying around the world when they should be at school or at home.

Lorna pouted and didn't instantly reply. She stared jealously at his phone. Kirby had confiscated hers when he suspended her from Hero.com after her involvement with Jake Hunter came to light. Toby had pleaded that she be allowed access again, but Kirby had been firm. In fact, the old man had been stubborn in his decision, claiming it was for her own good. Things were not helped when Chameleon started to suspect that she might have had something to do with Jake

The Message

Hunter's miraculous escape from the clutches of the Foundation, although it was impossible to prove anything. Nevertheless, an inquiry had been underway for a couple of months, and until it was resolved, Lorna was suspended.

Toby wanted to tell her all about the Moron Twins, but telling Lorna anything about his missions these days was like rubbing salt into a wound. She just sulked and avoided talking about his adventures. It was a shame as he and Lorna had become closer after sharing life-threatening missions.

'Em's going out of her mind,' said Lorna in a subdued voice. She stared straight ahead, refusing to look directly at her brother. 'She thinks she's located Pete and wants to go looking for him on her own.'

'That's nuts. Pete's not the person he used to be. Trust me on that, he tried to kill me several times.'

Lorna didn't reply. She knew just how twisted their old friend had become. Jake had told her how Pete had tried to kill Jake's parents by giving them an artificially created virus. How mixed up was he to do that? Jake had left out the details that Pete had been coerced into doing it, and that, in revenge, Jake had placed a time bomb virus into Pete.

'Still, she's probably going to do it. I wish I could help her.' She looked meaningfully at Toby. Emily still had access to Hero.com.

'You know there's nothing I can do about that.'

'Rubbish.'

'Honestly. If there was—'

'You always say that!'

'Because nothing's changed! Lorn, honestly, I don't need this right now.'

'Why? Because you're too busy ridding the world of all the bad guys?' She slammed her empty cola glass on the table. 'That's typical of you, you always wanted to be the perfect goodie-hero.'

'No, it's because something's not right at the Foundation.'

Lorna hesitated; there was an edge to Toby's voice. 'Why? What's happened?'

'Nothing specific. Not really. Chameleon is acting funny and they've just got me training up some cadets.'

'I thought you didn't mind doing that?'

'Not all the time! Lately I seem to be babysitting instead of going on real missions.' His voice dropped into a hushed whisper. 'I know where the Council of Evil is, Lorn. We could bring them down!'

Lorna studied her brother's face. His voice was filled with passion, and his expression was resolute. He had been held prisoner by the Council and tricked into working for them. That experience had angered him and he was determined to bring the bad guys down once and for all.

The Message

'See what I mean?' she said finally, arching an eyebrow.

'What?'

She mimicked Toby. 'We can bring down the Council of Evil and rid the world of all the nasty people!' Toby was surprised at her outburst. Lorna looked sullen. 'It's always about you and your massive plans. What about Emily and Pete? What about me?'

Toby sighed. 'I didn't mean it like that. I care about you guys . . . well, you and Em. I just don't understand why the Foundation is putting me and Jen on the sidelines.'

'There you go again! Now you're talking about your girlfriend,' said Lorna surlily.

'I wish,' muttered Toby before he sensed the derision in her tone. He sneered at her. 'I forgot, you only go for the insane megalomaniac villain types, don't you?' He regretted the words the moment he had said them.

Lorna stood up without a word and headed straight to the toilets. *To cry*, thought Toby with some satisfaction, although he didn't really believe that. Lorna was too strong, too stubborn. She just didn't want to be around him.

Toby scowled as he looked around the packed hall. He was sitting on his own again. That seemed to be a recurring theme in his life lately; nothing was going the way he had imagined.

Last week, he'd bought some goldfish in an attempt to cheer himself up. Fish were supposed to be relaxing, but even they had died from over-eating. Stupid fish. He couldn't even get that right.

Chameleon didn't look up as Kirby entered the control room. He was studying world maps overlaid with incident patterns of hyper-powered activity. They were all colour coded—yellow for past Council of Evil activity, blue for incidents in which Hero forces had been defeated, and red for ongoing Council activity. The board was smothered with colour, including the new addition of green blotches that marked incursions made by Forge. Green was starting to spread like an unwelcome fungus.

'The Council is getting stronger,' said Chameleon with concern. The last several months had seen his hatred for the enemy grow. His constant entanglements with Jake Hunter had made the war personal. Chameleon would die happy knowing that Hunter had been eradicated. 'And Forge is gathering strength.'

'Pete Kendall is leading them well,' commented Kirby. 'We have created a fine leader there.'

Chameleon scowled and shook his head. 'You've created a monster with the Kendall boy. It's about time you started to accept your responsibilities.'

The Message

Chameleon's tone was harsh and Kirby was visibly upset by the comment, but refrained from arguing. Since Jake had restored his own parents' memories and escaped from their clutches, Pete had become the leader of Forge, and Toby and Jen had saved the world from Lord Eon. All of this contributed to the deteriorating relationship between Chameleon and Kirby. Kirby suspected that Chameleon was making a play to take leadership of the Foundation. Today it was about to get worse.

'Professor Epstein has escaped,' said Kirby flatly.

Chameleon spun on his heels, his mouth ajar. 'How is that possible?'

Kirby shrugged and took a seat in front of the sleek computer that projected its displays on the air in front of them. He groaned as he took the weight from his old feet. 'I don't know, but he found a way out of the system during the procedure.'

'With Epstein you have created another deranged killer and then let him slip through your fingers? Sometimes I wonder which side you think we are on! Your methods are barbaric!'

'I didn't see you arguing when we used Jake Hunter's own sister to assassinate him,' countered Kirby.

Chameleon hissed. 'Well that's different . . . ' He knew that line of defence was feeble. 'And she wasn't an assassin. She was supposed to bring him in! He severed her hand and she got it into her own head that he was trying to kill her parents. That was all beyond my control.'

'Beyond your control? Yet it angers you when things extend beyond my grasp? That is very hypocritical, even for you. We can argue all day, but it won't change the fact Epstein is loose and has already started . . . abducting people.'

'Is that your polite euphemism for killing?'

'An eclectic mix of people are missing and we haven't any bodies. So far, there have been several top mathematicians and a dozen cryptographers. He's also taken six children while they were on their computers, gaming consoles or anything electrical. Thirty minutes ago we received this message.'

He tapped a key. A message replaced the world map:

74 72 61 70 70 65 64 . . . . . . NANOMITE LIVES! THE END OF DAYS IS COMING! 74 72 61 70 70 65 64

'It wasn't an email or SMS, it just appeared within the computer's operating system. Our programmers are trying to patch the system now in case he has hidden a malignant Trojan.'

'He's in our systems?' asked Chameleon in alarm.

'Not at the moment. We have locked everything

down and implemented the security protocols we created after Viral attacked our system. They didn't detect him the first time, but he won't get in a second time.'

Chameleon stared at the message. '"End of days", that's pretty biblical.'

'I think he is referring to us, humanity, rather than the world. After all, what good would a destroyed world be to him?'

'NanoMite? Is that what he's calling himself. What about these numbers?'

'Just junk characters, left-over code.'

'Where do we start looking for him?'

Kirby drummed his fingers on the desk and stared thoughtfully at the screen. 'Maybe we won't.'

'We can't let that fiend stay loose!'

'You misheard me; I said "we" won't. I want to send Toby out on the case. Let him build up the facts on his own.'

'You can't, he's training the cadets.'

'And he's doing a splendid job. You saw how the twins handled the incident in Canada?' It had been on all the news channels, the destruction was impossible to miss. The Foundation had praised the twins' quick thinking in rescuing the hostages and were not happy with Jen and Toby's handling of the subsequent arrest.

Chameleon's eyes narrowed. He liked Toby and could sense Kirby was planning something. 'Why not tell him the truth from the outset?'

'You know as well as I that Toby is a smart kid, but impulsive. He can sometimes jump to conclusions, both right and wrong. Sometimes it is better to set a small stone rolling to create an avalanche.'

'Why do I feel there is something you are not telling me?'

Kirby looked away, his gaze unfocused. It was as though he hadn't heard Chameleon. Chameleon continued:

'Toby's sister is a liability while she is still associating with Hunter. We need to put a stop to that.'

'I think that will resolve itself. It's always useful to have somebody so close to the enemy. It's Emily I worry about. She is becoming too much of a supporter of Pete's for my liking. You need to watch her. And, of course, Toby has his heart set on raiding the Council's island and I can't let that happen.'

'Why not? They're our enemy!'

'Because . . . because we can't,' snapped Kirby irritably. 'And should you become leader of this Foundation then you would know the reasons why! But for now I would prefer some fresh talent out there fighting for our cause. Toby will be better suited to tracking down Epstein, or NanoMite as he seems to prefer, and deleting him as quietly as possible and without my involvement.'

'I don't like this.'

'I'm not asking you to like it. I'm asking you to do it. Toby is our best agent. You should know; you trained him. Sometimes I think the Foundation would be better run in his hands.'

Chameleon scowled at the dig. 'What are you going to tell him about NanoMite?'

Kirby stood up and tapped his cane on the floor twice. It was a nervous habit.

'I shall tell him exactly what he needs to know. More or less.'

Yvonne Clayton arrived home late to her studio apartment. She was only twenty-two, but already one of the most impressive programmers at the Californian Institute of Technology, or CalTech, as was written across her sweatshirt.

She had her mobile phone wedged between her shoulder and ear as she locked the door behind her and headed for the refrigerator to empty the brown grocery bags of vegetables, hummus, and other disgustingly healthy foods.

'That's what I told him!' she squealed to her friend over the phone. 'I thought he wanted to—'

A high-pitched squeal suddenly emitted from the phone. She yelped and dropped it.

'Oh, heck . . . ' She trailed off, her anger at dropping her new phone overtaken by the shock of seeing a strange computerized face glaring at her from the screen. The room lights flickered. On impulse she hit the power button, blanking the screen, just in case she had a phone virus.

Then the power in her apartment went out with a loud clunk!

Cautiously, Yvonne pulled the kitchen curtain aside. The streetlights were still on—it was an outage only in her apartment block. She crossed to the cupboard under the sink; she was certain she had a torch in there.

The television suddenly switched on in the living room, scaring her. The lights were still off, the only illumination coming from the flickering TV. With her heart thumping, she slowly walked towards the lounge.

'H . . . hello?'

There was nobody there, just a political show playing to itself. Then the channel suddenly changed to a sitcom, the canned laughter sounding ominous in her dark apartment. Then it changed again and again, now cycling through the channels so rapidly that the images were a blur.

Yvonne's heart was racing. She was a rational thinker and didn't believe in ghosts or the supernatural, but

The Message

this was something out of her comfort zone. She ran to the power socket and yanked the cable out. The television died.

Before she could gather her thoughts, there was a heavy rattling noise from the kitchen. She snatched her landline phone and dialled 9-1 . . . her finger hovered over the final 1 for the emergency services.

'Who's there? I'm calling the cops!'

As if in answer the repetitive clattering grew in intensity. Yvonne edged towards the doorway and poked her head around the corner. Her refrigerator was violently rocking from side to side, lightning arcing along the power cable as the appliance edged further from the wall.

'Go away!' she screamed and thumbed the last 1 on the phone. She placed the phone to her ear . . . and was alarmed to discover the phone was dead. The telephone operated on a separate power supply from the rest of the building, so even if her electricity was cut, she still should get a dialling tone.

Then a voice spoke from the phone, an eerie electronic whisper that warbled in pitch. 'Yvonne Clayton, decryption specialist, CalTech, apartment 11030 South Sycamore Street . . . ' It reeled off her personal details without pause. Yvonne threw the phone down just as the refrigerator door swung open with a heavy thump and a figure climbed out of it!

The craziness of the situation suddenly flooded Yvonne with courage. 'OK, buster! What the hell are you doing in my fridge?'

The figure pulled itself to its full height and the courage she had summoned moments earlier fled. It was NanoMite in the weirdly smooth computer polygon form of Lord Destructo. He stared at his hand and dust seemed to fall away as the polygon armour vanished leaving a more realistic image beneath—it looked like a man, devoid of hair and impossibly thin. He wore a simulation of clothes, more like a burnt wetsuit. At first Yvonne thought his bones were showing through his chest, until she realized his rib cage was outside his chest, the bones scorched black and covered with tiny crawling nanite bugs.

The dust he had shaken off didn't fall to the ground; instead, it hovered like a mist before swishing in a controlled manner. It smothered the refrigerator. Yvonne was too stunned to even scream, as the fridge dissolved in front of her. The exterior panels went first, leaving just the shelves, food and the pump and freezing elements. In seconds they were gone too. The dust consumed everything right through to the plug in the wall. She couldn't help but notice that the creature seemed to gain strength from this, somehow becoming more *real*.

As the swarm started to consume her microwave, the creature stabbed a finger at her.

The Message

'Yvonne Clayton, you will be assimilated into my neural network!'

For a split second, Yvonne saw the cloud dart towards her and she felt as if a thousand pins were stabbing her skin. Then she fell into darkness.

It was well after midnight before the Wilkinsons left the party. Toby fell fast asleep as soon as his head touched the pillow. He was having the most wonderful dream before he was roughly shaken awake.

His instincts took over and he lashed out at the man shaking him. It took him seconds to realize he wasn't in danger—it was Chameleon.

Toby was puzzled. 'What are you doing here?'

'You didn't answer your phone!'

Toby groped for the alarm clock. 'It's four in the morning. I didn't hear it. I was having a great dream about . . . about . . . ' the images had vanished. 'Never mind.'

He reached for his phone. It wasn't there. He looked on the floor and under the bed. 'Where is it?'

'How should I know?'

Toby's search became more frantic. Anybody could access the powers on it. 'It was right here!'

'When did you last see it?'

'When I went to bed . . . ' Toby stopped himself. He

was still dressed because he had been exhausted when he returned home. He patted down his empty coat pockets as he tried to remember where he'd put it. 'I had it last night. I . . . '

He remembered putting it on the table at the party, but he was certain he had picked it up. Then he recalled Lorna eyeing it enviously. 'Oh, no!'

Toby ran from the room and bolted into Lorna's room. She wasn't there.

Chameleon appeared behind him. 'Lorna stole it?'

'Sssh,' whispered Toby. 'I don't want my parents to hear. They're not in the best mood. It looks like she did steal it.'

'We can track it and deactivate it. She won't get far.'

Toby shook his head. 'Lorn and Emily worked out how to turn that off ages ago.' In fact, he was with them when they stumbled across the option in the phone's tools. The tracking device was there to help them if they became stranded. They couldn't fathom a reason for having an option to turn it off, but now Toby knew. You disabled it if you wanted to fall off the grid and vanish.

'I'll look for her,' Chameleon assured him. 'I'll talk to Emily. She may know. But right now you have to meet up with Kirby. He needs your help.'

Toby groaned. 'I haven't slept! I'm shattered!'

'Evil doesn't sleep, Toby.'

The Message

* * *

Chameleon used his natural teleport ability to take them to a secure Foundation building. They appeared in a small room with a single door and a large glass screen that overlooked an obstacle course. Toby immediately recognized it as the War Room they used to train new cadets. He had been locked in here many times with Dumb and Dumber. Each time he had teleported in, so had never seen the building from the outside. In fact, he had no idea where it was actually located.

The obstacle course in the room constantly shifted so no two sessions were the same. Artificially Intelligent robots collectively call Nebulous—an assortment of tanks and tiny flying machines—downloaded watered-down powers from Hero.com and used them to simulate supervillain attacks. At the moment it was empty. Toby correctly guessed that, wherever the facility was located, it was probably night outside too.

Chameleon patted Toby on the shoulder. 'I must go and find Lorna. Please, for the sake of your sister, don't tell Kirby or anybody else what she has done.'

Toby nodded, although there was nothing more he would have liked to do at that moment than land his sister in trouble. Chameleon left the room, leaving Toby alone with his thoughts. He was just wondering what Jen was doing, when the door opened and Kirby entered.

'Ah! Toby, my boy. So good to see you!'

Toby stared at the old man. 'Quark,' he snapped.

Kirby smiled. 'That would be "supernova".'

Toby sighed with relief. A Kirby impostor had duped him before in the Council of Evil. Ever since he had a series of keywords to verify he was talking to the real man.

'I heard about your cadets in Toronto,' said Kirby.

Inwardly, Toby groaned. He was expecting to be berated for that. 'Yes, about that . . . '

'They were wonderful! You've done a good job training them up.'

Toby's face froze in surprise. 'I have?'

'Completely. That's why I want to spirit you away on a little side project. A manhunt.'

Toby was instantly suspicious. To be woken up at four in the morning for an 'urgent' mission was a little more than a side project. 'I thought after I'd trained them up that we would be heading for the Council of Evil headquarters?'

'That can wait.'

Toby was petulant, but he was tired of the constant excuses to avoid his plan. 'No it can't!'

'Toby, it can and it will. The Council are not going anywhere, but our target is.'

The Message

Toby was angry with Kirby for changing the agreement. The whereabouts of the Council's headquarters was a closely guarded secret. Toby had been imprisoned there. The Council had tricked him into doing their dirty work; actions that could have brought the world under the villains' control. Toby had never forgiven himself for allowing that to happen. However, it had given him first-hand experience of why the Council of Evil needed to be destroyed. He had managed to escape with the island's coordinates and had presented them to Kirby thinking that it would be the ideal opportunity for the Foundation to smash its rival. However, Kirby had been strangely reluctant. Despite this, part of him was curious about what was more important than ridding the world of the evil organization once and for all. 'Who is it?'

Kirby called up the same text he had shown Chameleon.

'NanoMite,' said Toby. 'Does that mean he is really small?'

'No, it means he controls nanites. It's nanotechnology. They're very small robots, some are atoms across, that can bond together to form bigger objects, even complex machines which we call *nanobots*. There are nanites that cut, others that bond, some are even microfactories that recycle atoms they encounter. By adjusting atoms, electrons, and so on, these machines can

01101000010000101001010011001001100101

turn wood into metal. Sand into electrical components. They feed from power lines and can suck electricity from batteries as if it was moisture in the air! While they are in the vicinity your phone and other electronic devices won't work. It's a good early warning system.

'NanoMite has command of several billion of those micro-machines. Our one advantage is that he doesn't possess the ability to replicate the nanites themselves. The machines can turn one substance into another, or control bigger machines, but they can't self-replicate or create new life. If he could replicate, then . . . ' a dark expression clouded Kirby's face. He didn't need to finish the sentence.

Kirby replaced the message with a series of photographs: six young children, ranging in age from nine to fifteen, and dozens of adults. 'All these people were taken from their homes without any visible signs of entry. In some instances electronic devices had been destroyed or had even disappeared completely.'

'Who are they?'

'All random people. All dead. The children were all playing computer games at the time. The adults are all mathematical or computer geniuses.'

'Where were their bodies found?' asked Toby.

'We haven't found them.'

'So how do you know they are dead?'

The Message

Kirby pondered the question; it hadn't crossed his mind. 'Good point. In which case we have a lot of kidnapping cases and no motive.'

'So who is NanoMite? One of the COE's new psychopaths?'

Kirby hesitated. 'A professor; I didn't know him. He was once a brilliant scientist who experimented on nanotechnology. I want you and Jen to examine the last victim's apartment. See if you can discover why he's taking these people.'

The mention of Jen's name suddenly made a boring mission sound a little more fun. 'When do we start?'

'Right now. Jen is already at the crime scene waiting for you.'

At that moment the observation screen loudly cracked. Both Kirby and Toby jumped and spun to face the window. Toby could feel a wave of heat from it and watched in astonishment as the glass suddenly melted like ice.

Beyond, he could see dozens of machines under the Nebulous's control—ranging from small caterpillar tracked tanks to small airborne devices that hovered on the spot—all pointing their way. Their weapons glowed with energy, powers sucked from Hero.com.

'What's going on?'

The room lights suddenly flickered. Kirby unsheathed his sword from his cane and hunkered for action.

'You'd better download some powers, lad. I think NanoMite has left a little welcoming gift for us.'

Toby's hand went for his phone . . . before he remembered that he didn't have it. The flying killing machines suddenly swooped into the room, weapons blazing and coordinated by an Artificially Intelligent computer that specialized in combat.

And Toby had no superpowers to fend them off.

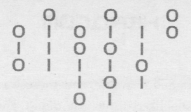

The First Wave

Emily stared at herself in the mirror. She clipped the fringe of her bobbed blonde hair back, and saw the fear reflected in her eyes. She forced herself to calm down.

'Are you sure you're going to be OK?' said Lorna, sitting on the edge of the bed.

Emily nodded and forced a smile. 'Sure. We know what we're doing, right?'

This made Lorna laugh, although she wasn't feeling particularly happy. 'At least let's pretend we do!' She became serious again. 'Like you said, if we don't sort out this mess, nobody else will.'

The 'mess' she was referring to was Jake Hunter and Pete Kendall. The very people Toby no longer seemed to care about. Lorna had been . . . dating, for want of a better word, Jake, before she discovered he was downloading powers from Villain.net and was known in the Foundation files as the Dark Hunter. As with all these things, the clue was in the title. Jake had always been nice to her . . . well, maybe not exactly nice, but certainly bearable, and there was something about him she liked. She just didn't know what it was.

Pete was a friend. He had been Toby's best mate until they had argued over how best to use Hero.com. A deep rift had developed between the two, something they hadn't been able to resolve before Pete was plunged into vats of raw superpowers—the super equivalent of being dumped in sewage. He had fallen into a coma, only to be awoken from it after being pre-programmed by Jake and the Council of Evil. They had tapped into Pete's negative emotions and used them to create a rampaging supervillain.

Pete's body had developed a method of processing his absorbed superpowers so he was able to combine them to create new ones. It was a gift he shared with Jake; although Pete could only combine powers he had soaked up whereas Jake could create new, previously unseen, ones.

Because they were the only two supers who could do this, both the Foundation and the Council wanted them as a super-weapon. Jake had decided to side with the Council, whereas Pete, typically, didn't know what he wanted and had ended up leading Forge.

All of this had occurred while Emily had been out of the picture as a prisoner of Lord Eon. When she had returned and was debriefed, she had been shocked at just how complicated things had become in her absence.

In an effort to set things right, she had been trying to liaise with Pete and Lorna, keeping under the Foundation's radar. Chameleon's unannounced visit a few hours ago had alarmed her. He bombarded her with questions about Lorna's whereabouts.

Emily thought she had coolly deflected his prying questions, but wasn't happy about lying. She was supposed to be a hero. Then again, Chameleon had acted rather oddly, as if he was on edge and under pressure. Once he had left, she had agreed with Lorna that now was the time to act.

Emily looked at Lorna through the mirror. 'Do you think he'll listen to me?'

'Em, you know he will. Pete always listened to you. Since he and Toby fought there's no chance they'll try and talk to one another again, and Eric Kirby isn't interested in helping either of them. Not any more.'

Emily knew her friend was right. It was up to them to sort things out and get things back to the way they used to be. It had taken her weeks to contact Pete. She had used all the resources in the Foundation computer systems just to get an approximate location. Once she had established contact with Forge, she had been sent to many different locations around the world, quantum tunnelling to each one only to discover that it was yet another relay point. Finally she had managed to secure an appointment with her old pal.

Lorna mused how odd it was that a series of seemingly unconnected events had led them here—a lightning strike to their telegraph pole that connected them to Hero.com; holding the supervillain, Basilisk, prisoner in Pete's shed and Pete's subsequent kidnapping that coincided with his parents separating; Mr Grimm's duplicitous plan to launch Forge against the world by using Jake as their key weapon; and even Toby and Pete's tumble back in time to save Eric Kirby, in which Pete had innocently sewn the idea of Hero.com. They were all chance occurrences, a chaotic jumble of incidents that had affected their lives and created their current situations.

'And you'll be OK with Jake?' asked Emily. 'You don't want me to come along?'

Lorna shook her head. 'We have an understanding. Besides, he owes me one after I helped him escape from the hospital. I think I can persuade him to leave the Council of Evil. That's not who he is.'

Emily looked at her friend with curiosity. 'You still haven't told me how you're able to download again.'

'I have my ways,' smiled Lorna. She thought the fewer people who knew about what she had done, the better. 'Shall we go . . . or shall we keep on stalling?'

The First Wave

They had been bolstering each other's courage for the last thirty minutes, anything rather than actually do the job.

Emily nodded firmly. 'OK. Let's go.'

They departed on their private quests, unaware that their every move had been monitored, analysed and recorded.

Toby threw himself headfirst through the door as Nebulous's aerial drones opened fire behind him with a barrage of superpowers—laser vision, heat rays, and energy volleys tore up the floor.

Kirby sliced one of the drones in half with a skilful sword slash. Despite his age, he was fast. He somersaulted over the explosion and into the corridor.

Behind them, the tanks, downloading levitation powers from the Hero.com server, climbed up the walls and into the observation booth, their caterpillar tracks sliding through the puddles of warm liquid glass.

Toby and Kirby raced down the corridor. Ahead, a blast door suddenly slammed closed, trapping them.

'Shoot it open!' ordered Kirby.

'I can't! I don't have any powers!' snapped Toby. He was usually calm in times of crisis, but he felt vulnerable without any powers at his disposal.

'Where's your phone?'

01010000010010010010010011101

Toby hesitated, remembering Chameleon's comment about not revealing Lorna had taken it. 'I left it at home.' He felt the irony of being within one of the Foundation's many facilities and unable to access Hero.com, the very website that held the Foundation together.

The battle tanks rounded a corner and whirled towards them, lightning erupting from the swivelling weapons turret. Kirby extended his hand; a scintillating energy shield blocked the corridor and absorbed the lightning. The multiple impacts were so severe, his feet slid backwards on the smooth floor; the strain of keeping the shield up showed on his face.

Toby tried to prise the doors open, but he couldn't get his fingers in the narrow rim between the two halves. He waved at the security camera mounted in the corner of the corridor, and was dismayed to see the power light suddenly switched off as Nebulous seized control of the system.

Four tanks now blocked the corridor. Toby looked desperately around for a weapon. He might not have superpowers, but he was still smarter than a machine . . . he hoped.

'Get down!' shouted Toby as he suddenly grappled Kirby to the floor.

'What!' exclaimed Kirby as Toby pulled him down. Kirby's energy shield fizzled out as another volley of

The First Wave

lightning bolts arced overhead and melted a hole in the centre of the door.

Toby took some satisfaction from the fact that his plan had worked. 'Let's go!'

He jumped through the narrow hole. Kirby followed him as the tanks switched powers to laser pulses. A ragged section of door fell away under the new onslaught, but Toby and Kirby were already running down another length of corridor. They passed the lifts and Toby stabbed a button, he knew the War Room was located underground.

'No use! Nebulous will control them!' said Kirby, fighting for his breath. 'Head for the stairs.'

They made it to the fire escape door as the tanks rounded another corner. Toby could feel his hair sizzle as the lasers narrowly missed his skull.

The fire escape was bland and functional and by the time they reached the first landing, the tanks were already on their heels. The caterpillar tracks made short work of ascending the stairs. More aerial drones buzzed in pursuit.

Toby bounded up two steps at a time, but was alarmed to see Kirby was lagging behind, increasingly fighting for his breath.

'Are you OK?' Kirby nodded, but his face was bright red. 'How many more floors?'

'Ten,' gasped Kirby.

A laptop-sized drone suddenly shot up the staircase, borne on mechanical dragonfly wings. To Toby, it looked like a fascinating combination of a helicopter and an insect, but right now he didn't have time to admire the design. A miniature gun barrel swivelled to face him.

Toby snatched a fire extinguisher off the wall and slogged the machine. The drone exploded in a tiny fire-ball, the wreckage rolling down the staircase and under the tread of a battle tank as it rounded onto the land-ing. The tank's weapons immediately targeted Toby.

Toby fired the extinguisher; bilious white foam cov-ered the tank and the one behind. It was enough to blind the tank's sensors. The machines shot a wild vol-ley of apple-sized fireballs in Toby's direction but he was already pounding up the stairs. The blind rear tank only succeeded in blowing up the leader machine, blocking the stairs and buying the heroes time.

The short rest had rejuvenated Kirby, although he still remained several steps behind. Ahead lay a fire exit. Toby crashed through the barrier and into darkness.

Kirby heaved the fire door shut; not that it would hold the machines off for long.

'Now what?' said Toby between breaths.

The landscape around him was lit by a plump full moon. They were standing in a rough car park. The floor was not tarmac, but dry desert gravel. A dozen cars were parked under a rocky ridge. Toby ran to the top of a rocky incline and stopped dead in his tracks.

'Where are we?' he asked in awe.

The moonlit landscape that stretched out before him looked like a lunar surface. Massive craters scarred the desert. It looked completely alien.

'The Nevada desert,' said Kirby as he made for a pick-up truck. The keys were still in the ignition: this was usually a zero-crime area.

'What are those craters?'

'This used to be the US military's nuclear test range, the Nevada Test Site. Now, unless you can fly to safety, get in!' He turned the engine over.

Toby couldn't tear his gaze from the unearthly vista. Each of the hundreds of craters that stretched into the distance represented a detonated nuclear bomb. It was unreal.

'Toby!'

The fire escape door—attached to a small building that looked more like a port-a-loo than the entrance to a top-secret Foundation training room—blew open and a foam-covered tank sprang out, followed by a flock of flying killers. Toby darted for the pick-up truck as Kirby reversed it.

The tank fired—blowing up two cars as it tracked the pick-up truck. Had its sensors not been clogged, the pick-up would have been destroyed with the first shot.

Toby jumped into the back of the vehicle and Kirby accelerated onto a barren stretch of road. Toby watched as more Nebulous-controlled machines spilled into the desert, but they didn't give chase, instead they milled around the parked vehicles. He saw a cloud of spores detach from the tanks and drones and start to devour the vehicles. The chassis were dissolved as easily as a swarm of locusts eating their way through a cornfield.

Toby slid the pick-up's rear window open and shouted to Kirby inside. 'Is that NanoMite?'

'No, that's just something he left as a booby trap. A batch of nanites that he left in the system to hack into Nebulous. He'll control those nanites though through some remote access.'

'Who is he? How did he get into the Foundation's systems?'

Kirby didn't answer immediately in case he said the wrong thing. 'That's what I need you to find out. What is more important is that you find a way to stop him and his Swarm at any cost. We'll head to the nearest city and get help there. I just hope that nanite Swarm doesn't follow us.'

'What about the people in the facility?'

'The machines were coming for us. Specifically, me. I think the others will be safe if they keep their heads down and evacuate.'

The First Wave

'Why is NanoMite coming after you?'

Kirby didn't answer. He crunched through the gears, pressing the vehicle as fast as it would go along the dirt road. Toby clung on in the back, watching the pock-marked landscape pass by and marvelling at the sheer destructive force required to scar the landscape.

He hoped the nano-Swarm wouldn't follow them. Entering combat without his powers had been a frightening experience, and not one he was willing to try again.

Hayden stared at the platter of ham and sausages his twin had just laid on the table.

'What is this?'

Jurgen sat at the table and eagerly began eating. 'Lunch!' he said, spraying food at his brother.

Hayden winced, not wishing to be spat on again. He pushed the plate away.

'Jurg, I'm a vegetarian. Or a fishitarian . . . 'cause I can eat fish too. Just not meat.'

Jurgen never once stopped chewing as he stared at Hayden. 'You don't want?'

'No, I don't want.' Hayden sighed, how could identical twins be so different? Their parents had split up when they were younger. The twins were raised without any knowledge of one another. It was when they both were approached by the Hero Foundation to try Hero.com that they discovered the truth.

Now, even though their dad had died, leaving Hayden to fend for himself, and they lived on separate continents, they could now regularly see one another thanks to downloadable superpowers.

Jurgen was angry with his mother for keeping such a secret, but had no clue how he could tell her that they had found one another again, without revealing their super-secret.

'Do you have any vegetables?' Hayden asked hopefully.

His brother laughed and reached for the fruit bowl, handing him a brown banana. Their mobile phones suddenly chimed in unison. Jurgen ignored his and continued eating. Hayden read the text message.

'Dude, we have a mission!'

Jurgen gave a reluctant sigh. 'More training.' He was getting tired of the relentless exercises. It felt like being back at school, and to make it worse, their teacher was younger than him.

Hayden shook his head. 'No, this is the real deal! We don't have any training wheels!' He jumped to his feet; the excitement made him forget all about his hunger. He slapped his brother on his arm to hurry him up. 'Come on, bro. We've got a world to save!'

He slid through the on-screen superpower options

and selected his three favourites. The screen pulsed, optically transferring the power into him. He felt the immediate rush of energy.

'I love being a superhero!' he chuckled, performing a little jig of excitement.

The only thing good about being a super, is going to cool places, thought Toby as he stared down at the wild neon of Las Vegas Boulevard. They had hit the Vegas suburbs in just under two hours. Whatever time it was now, the famous city was showing no signs of winding down.

Then he corrected himself, he currently wasn't a super, but a regular kid, until he could access the Internet.

They passed the huge Bellagio Hotel; the lake in front was throwing up a wonderful fountain display. Opposite was the Eiffel Tower, or rather a smaller five-eighths-scale version that belonged to the splendid Paris Las Vegas Hotel. Toby was enthralled; the danger from the last couple of hours was almost forgotten. Kirby stopped the truck.

'Are we going inside?' he asked hopefully.

Kirby shot him a scornful glance. 'We haven't got time to play! Sometimes, Toby, I wonder where your head is at.'

The blunt dig hurt Toby's feelings, but he refused to let Kirby notice. Ever since Pete had switched sides, Toby had the distinct feeling that Kirby blamed him. He'd never actually said that, but it was becoming clear that Toby was no longer his favourite Downloader.

Toby jumped from the back of the pick-up, and landed awkwardly, spraining his ankle.

'OW! Dammit!' He hobbled, taking the weight off his foot. It was the first time he'd been properly injured in a long while. He had been shot at, frozen, blasted into the lower atmosphere, dropped from great heights, bounced through time and assaulted in a variety of other ways, but because he had had his powers, the injuries didn't seem quite real. Now, a simple sprain was agony.

Kirby wasn't watching him, he was anxiously looking at his mobile phone. He suddenly looked across at the Eiffel Tower. Moments later Hayden and Jurgen dodged between the lines of taxis entering the hotel. They looked fresh and alert, reminding Toby that he hadn't slept properly and fatigue was clouding his decisions.

'Yo, Bossman!' beamed Hayden. 'Tobe-meister!'

'Mister Kirby, Tony,' said Jurgen somewhat more respectfully, although he had yet to get Toby's name right.

'Glad to see you, boys!' said Kirby with a relieved

smile. Toby felt a twinge of jealousy: it was clear, at least to him, that the twins were his replacements. 'I can't raise Chameleon. Have you heard from him?'

'Radio silence, boss. Last I heard was that he was going after Dark Hunter, big time.'

Kirby looked anxious. 'He's making a habit of disappearing without a trace,' he muttered. 'Never mind. We have a crisis at the War Room. We have been attacked by nanites—'

'Nanna-whats?' asked Hayden with a frown.

Toby interjected. He thought he'd better say something in case people started regarding him as a fifth-wheel. 'Nanites are microscopic robots that can do a variety of tasks. Alone they are not a threat, but thousands or billions of them can form together and cause a lot of trouble.'

Kirby nodded in agreement. 'And these nanites are acting as a Swarm with one mind. They have corrupted Nebulous's artificial intelligence and will be using that as advanced tactical combat knowledge. But they are being commanded from somewhere else.'

'Who is the perpetrator behind all of this?' asked Jurgen. He was still chewing a sausage he had brought with him.

'That's what Toby is going to find out. You boys are going to go back to the War Room and stop the Swarm.'

Toby tapped Kirby on the shoulder.

'They don't have to go back there.' He pointed down the street. 'The War Room has come to us.'

Everybody turned as a chorus of car horns started up. A six-metre nanobot had appeared at the crossroads. It was human in shape, a mishmash of War Room technology: the cars in the car park and other odds and ends. Its arms bristled with multiple weapons from the War Room drones.

A taxi slammed into the foot of the creature, steam rising from under the bonnet. The driver hurried out as the robot pointed at the vehicle. A stream of nanites fired out, enveloping the taxi. In seconds the bodywork disintegrated, leaving the chassis, engine, and wiring underneath. A few seconds later, that vanished too.

Toby noticed patches of yellow appear across the robot's body and he realized that the machine hadn't destroyed the taxi—it had absorbed it. He opened his mouth to tell the others, but Hayden and Jurgen had already taken to the air. He noticed Kirby was running for cover. Typical, Primes always thought they were more valuable than Downloaders because they had been born with inherent powers. Toby took a few steps after the twins, but his ankle hurt like mad.

'No wait! You don't know what you're doing!'

Crowds of people were now fleeing from the

nanobot as it demolished the traffic around it. Few people paid any heed to the two figures flying towards the danger.

'This is gonna be wicked!' screamed Hayden. He orbited the robot and unleashed several fireballs from the palms of his hands. The giant rocked as they struck, the flames sizzling across its body.

'Jurg! Go in low, let's trip this metal-head over!'

Jurgen peeled away and circled around the back of the machine as it turned to swat his brother. He flew over a cloud of nanites as they chewed through more vehicles, transporting the microscopic particles back to the nanobot's body.

Jurgen opened his mouth and belched a cone of ice on the floor behind the robot. It was a favourite tactic of the twins—fire and ice. They were convinced it would stop almost everything. All Hayden had to do was blast the machine with enough force that it would trip on the slick road . . . before it melted.

Hayden hovered in the air to get the nanobot's attention. A dozen guns, attached along the machine's arms, all rotated towards him—every one firing a distinctly different energy power.

Hayden wasn't prepared for the multicoloured barrage. He dodged as best he could, calling up a protective shield around him to take the brunt of the assault. The attack was too strong, and the bubble burst, propelling him out of control against the Eiffel Tower. He hit it with such force that he wedged between the girders, knocking his head hard, sending him unconscious.

'Hayden!' bellowed Jurgen as he saw his brother swatted away. Jurgen tried to fly up to the robot's eye level to blind it—but the monster was growing. At first, Jurgen was confused, then he looked down to see nanites swirling around the robot's feet like a tornado, sucking in any form of technology, transferring it to the nanobot to make it bigger.

Jurgen was so spellbound he didn't notice the mighty metal palm swat him from the sky. He spiralled down, splashing into the Bellagio's lake.

The fleeing crowds buffeted Toby. He watched with despair as the robot stomped across the boulevard, kicking a bus out of its way—which was consumed by the nano-cloud moments later. The robot increased in size with every step it took as it lumbered towards the Eiffel Tower. At first, Toby thought it was going for Hayden, but as the machine reached out, a cloud of nanites leapt from its hands and started eating the steel girders.

The robot was feeding off the tower! It wasn't just absorbing the metal, its nanites broke down wiring, bulbs, everything and anything it could recycle. There was no telling how big it would get.

The First Wave

Toby looked around for something—anything—he could use. Then he spotted a mobile phone lying on the ground, dropped by somebody too panicked to care. He scooped it up and excitedly tried to access Hero.com on the mobile browser . . . but he couldn't find the site. With a sinking feeling he remembered that entering the URL was not enough, the website was hidden behind a constantly changing alphanumeric string. He wouldn't be getting any powers from there.

The nanobot shook as it grew. The top of the Eiffel Tower dissolved like sand, spreading quickly down to where Hayden was wedged ninety-one metres up and unconscious. If the tower dissolved around him he would plummet to his death.

Toby started to run, unsure if he could do anything to stop the attack. His ankle ached with every step, forcing him to stop. The robot was getting bigger from the components within the stolen tower, and time was running out. Then a crazy thought struck him. When weighed against doing nothing, it was worth a try. He rushed back to the pick-up truck. Luckily Kirby had left the keys in the ignition. He hopped in and switched the engine on.

He had tried to drive a Porsche once in Germany, and that had gone terribly wrong, but after watching his dad sedately drive the family car, he thought he knew why. He carefully pressed down on the clutch with his sore foot and pushed the gear stick into first. The gears crunched but the stick moved into place. Then he stomped on the accelerator as he released the clutch pedal.

The pick-up lunged forward with a peculiar noise—Toby realized that the handbrake was still on. He pushed it down and the truck hurtled forward, the engine redlining. He floored the clutch again and moved into second gear with another nasty crunch, but at least the engine didn't stall.

He aimed straight for the nanobot as it grew an additional five metres. Luckily the roads were empty: pedestrians had fled to safety and every other vehicle had been absorbed.

He pushed the accelerator flush against the floor—and suddenly wondered if the vehicle had airbags. His hand snapped for the seatbelt, but it refused to move as the inertia locks gripped it tight.

It was too late to worry now. The colossus filled the windscreen.

Hayden drifted back into consciousness—and immediately wished he hadn't. The nanobot was looming over him, twice as large as when he first attacked it. A quick glance up revealed the top of the tower was missing. He felt the girder under his hand suddenly go pliable—then it collapsed into a cloud of steel filings that got sucked into the robot like a Hoover. Hayden fell.

He kicked in his flying power to break his fall, and zoomed away to safety—it was then that he noticed the pick-up truck racing towards the nanobot, its engine straining. He mistakenly assumed the driver was in peril.

'No way! I'll save ya!'

Hayden blasted the ground in front of the pick-up, forming a crater in the road. One side of the pick-up rolled into the crater—the entire vehicle suddenly rolled onto its roof. He watched as the truck rolled several times before coming to a halt upside-down, horn blaring. He had hoped the vehicle would just come to a stop in the crater.

'Oops! Sorry!'

He swooped down. The driver was pinned in his seat by an airbag. Hayden tugged the door, but it was buckled and wouldn't open.

'You're lucky I was in the neighbourhood, my friend. A head on run-in with that thing would have killed ya.' He formed a ping-pong sized fireball and blasted the door off its hinges. He was feeling proud about mastering the little techniques Toby had showed him. 'I just saved your life!'

Hayden pulled the driver out—and was surprised to

receive a punch across the face for his troubles. He staggered backwards and was shocked to discover it was Toby.

'You moron!' Toby screamed. 'You almost killed me!'

'I was trying to save your life!'

'By shooting me?'

'What were you trying to do?'

Toby was about to answer, but caught sight of the nanobot. It was now twenty metres tall and finishing off the last of the Tower. Then it started on consuming the casino that lay at the foot of the Tower.

Jurgen joined them, patting his twin's shoulders. 'You are OK?' Hayden nodded. Jurgen spun Toby round in concern. 'And, Tony, you are good too?'

Toby pointed at his pick-up truck. 'Jurg, can you lift this?'

'This? *Ja*,' said Jurgen, easily lifting the pick-up over his head.

Toby was relieved the twins insisted on downloading the same powers every time. 'Good. Now throw it straight at the nanobot's body. Aim for the chest and throw it as hard as you can!'

Jurgen was an excellent athlete, and loved field events, specializing in javelin. He balanced the heavy pick-up on one hand, took a short run and hurled the vehicle.

It was a perfect shot. The pick-up hit the nanobot in

the centre of its back and pushed through the chest—
arcing out the other side and crashing into the casino
below.

The impact was so severe that the component parts
of the robot separated. The impact shockwave rippled
through the machine, forcing the tiny nanites to release
their hold on the accumulated junk. The hundreds of
thousands of tiny components that were held together
suddenly crashed to the floor in piles of twisted junk
metal. Within seconds the entire beast had shuddered
apart, leaving nothing more than a pile of junk.

'Wow!' shouted Hayden, punching the air. 'That was
mega-awesome! How did you know?'

Toby beamed with satisfaction. 'Goldfish.' The twins
gave him a funny look. 'Goldfish don't stop eating.
They can die from over-eating. Just like that thing. It
was getting bigger and bigger, absorbing everything it
could, but there were still the same number of
nanobots holding it together. Kirby said they couldn't
multiply. So in the end they were stretched too thin,
too weak. That's why I was going to drive into it.'

Jurgen clapped him on the back, knocking the breath
from him. 'That was very clever, Tony.'

Toby allowed himself a brief moment of victory
before Kirby ran over from his hiding place. Toby was
angry that Kirby, like all Primes, thought himself too
valuable for direct confrontations. He dismissed that

thought. He had seen Kirby fight when the chips were down and he owed his new life to him. It might be one without his best friend Pete, but it was without doubt a rare opportunity he was thankful for.

'Jurgen, you were amazing!' cried Kirby. Toby suddenly felt the elation sucked from him. 'I saw what you did. Good thinking!'

Toby stared at Jurgen, waiting for him to point out it was all his idea. Instead Jurgen grinned and accepted the hearty handshake from Kirby.

'It was nothing,' Jurgen simpered. 'My brother sets them up, I bring them down,' he said, pounding his chest for emphasis.

Toby was furious. Before he could say anything he suddenly caught movement in the destruction—the nanite-Swarm was swirling, still active. He was about to shout out—but Jurgen had seen the problem too.

The German rushed forward, his mouth as wide as possible. Ice erupted like a geyser, freezing the Swarm in a huge block of ice that crashed to the ground. It was over in seconds, every nanite had been trapped.

Toby hated himself for admitting that was a good idea. Jurgen and Hayden hi-fived each other, and Kirby shook them both by the shoulders ecstatically. Nobody congratulated Toby.

'You're both geniuses!' laughed Kirby.

The sound of approaching sirens broke Kirby from

The First Wave

his revelry. He turned to Toby and handed him his phone.

'Here, use this until you get your own back. Find Jen, she's waiting for you at the crime scene. We better go before the authorities start asking awkward questions.' He gripped the twins' arms and all three teleported away with a boom.

Toby stood in the ruined boulevard alone. He was seething with anger and jealousy. Why had Jurgen simply not told the truth? Was he one of those egotists who craved attention, or was he simply not used to praise and got it where he could. Toby recalled training them. He had been tough on the twins, mainly because he felt training the new kids was beneath him. He couldn't think of a time he had congratulated either of them. He must look like an impossible-to-please teacher. Then something else occurred to him: the twins probably hated him, just as he hated school teachers who constantly spouted and complained.

Doubt started encroaching on Toby's thoughts. He remembered both Lorna and Pete accusing him of being arrogant because he wouldn't allow them to exploit their powers for money. Pete had even called him a control freak. Toby was starting to see why. Was he really responsible for alienating everybody? Was he acting so arrogantly that he couldn't see how much he was annoying people?

Feeling fragile, Toby called up the re-downloaded teleport power built into Kirby's phone. He made a mental image of his destination so he could teleport there. That was easy, all he had to do was think of Jen.

At least she liked him.

The Hunt Begins

'What kept you?' asked Jen irritably.

Toby's smile vanished as he teleported into the room. Jen stood arms akimbo, an impatient look on her face.

Toby's reply was dry. 'I was busy saving Las Vegas from a horde of micro-machines.'

Jen grunted in response as if it was the worst excuse she'd heard. 'I was asleep, you know, before I was dragged here. I need my beauty sleep.'

Toby couldn't avoid a lingering glance. Even in a hastily thrown on sweatshirt and with her hair in a messy ponytail, he wanted to say that she didn't. Luckily he stopped himself; that sounded so lame in his head. He kept lying to himself about having a crush, and now he was reaping the consequences—he felt doubly depressed that she was irritated with him.

'Like it's my fault we're both here!' he said, looking around the apartment. 'Wherever *here* is.'

Jen sighed, a little too theatrically. 'Don't you read your messages?' She waggled her phone at him.

'I didn't get it,' he mumbled. He didn't want to

admit his own sister had stolen his phone. As angry as he was with Lorna, he didn't want to turn other people's opinions against her.

'You're useless.' It was a flippant comment and she smiled as she said it, but it hurt Toby. Jen read from the device. 'This is the home of Yvonne Clayton, a promising student at CalTech. She specialized in cryptology.'

'Is that something to do with crosswords?' said Toby glibly as he looked around the apartment. It was a nice place, equipped with a huge TV and every type of media player he could name. Yvonne clearly loved her gadgets.

'It's the study of codes, moron. Apparently she was one of the best students they'd ever seen. A keen programmer too.'

'And how did she go missing?'

'That's the reason I got dragged out of bed.'

'Kirby mentioned a new villain, NanoMite. I saw some of his handiwork in Vegas. He can control nanites—they're miniature robots—'

'Duh! I know what they are. They're artificially created microscopic machines.'

Toby scowled. She was treating him exactly the way he had treated the twins. 'That's about all we know.' He examined the door. It had been kicked open; wooden splinters were strewn over the floor. 'I guess he broke in through here.'

The Hunt Begins

Jen rolled her eyes and puffed loudly. 'That was the police, who forced entry after neighbours reported a scuffle.' She waggled her phone again. 'It's all in the report. You should read it.'

'Why? You're doing such a patronizing job at reading it out.'

Jen pursed her lips and slid the phone into her pocket. 'Sorry, but I get cranky with no sleep. So, Einstein, how did Nano get in and out with the woman?'

Toby looked around for any clues. He walked into the kitchen and stopped in his tracks.

'The fridge has gone,' he said looking at the empty space. 'And the microwave too.'

Jen followed him in. 'Who are you all of a sudden? Sherlock Holmes? Maybe she didn't have them? Or are you saying our villain stole them too?'

Toby ignored her and examined the fridge space closely. He traced his fingers over scuffs on the wall and deep indentations on the floor where the refrigerator had danced out when it shook.

'Anyone with the state-of-the-art stuff in her apartment would have a decent fridge and microwave.'

'You know, some people can cook fresh. They don't have to nuke everything.'

'You're right. That's why she bought a bunch of fresh things, including a tub of ice cream that was to go in the freezer.' He pointed to an empty grocery bag, and another that hadn't yet been emptied and sported a wet patch from where the ice cream had melted.

Jen was impressed, but tried to hide it. Toby then pointed at the indentations on the floor.

'The fridge was moving, maybe like somebody was trapped inside. You can see the scuff marks on the wall as it rocked from side-to-side.'

'They could have been made when she moved in.'

Toby flicked the torn wallpaper. 'Too fresh. These marks on the floor were made as the fridge rocked out of the bay. See? Little circles like the screw legs you get on a fridge to set it level.'

'So she was attacked by her fridge,' said Jen sceptically. 'Which then kidnapped her?'

'The apartment door was locked from the inside. You said so.' Toby was thinking hard. 'It was obviously Nano-Mite who did this. He must be able to move through the electricity cables, that's how he's getting in!'

'And he came through the fridge?'

'Why not? I'm guessing that one electrical appliance is just as good as another. Kirby told me some kids were abducted when they were playing games. He came out of the screen!'

'Whoa, wait up. How can he move through wires?'

Toby was wondering why Kirby hadn't just told them the facts from the beginning. Why had he wanted them to visit the crime scene? 'The machines in the War

The Hunt Begins

Room were infected by nanites. Kirby was convinced NanoMite left them behind. If they're small enough, and I'm talking microns across,' he paused to allow Jen to ask what a micron was. He was disappointed when she just signalled for him to continue, 'then I guess it's possible that those nanites can also get through systems . . . flowing along with the rest of the current.'

'I'm no expert on nanotechnology, but is it really possible to make machines that small?'

'Maybe not for ordinary science . . . but the Foundation or the Council? It is possible. I did it myself. That's how I escaped from the Council's island and found you in Chicago.'

'OK, let's suppose for a minute that NanoMite can digitize himself into computers—'

'Not just computers; machines. Any machine. Like the fridge.'

Jen nodded, it made some sort of sense. 'So he digitized this woman and escaped through the microwave?'

Toby shrugged. 'Something like that. I think it's more like the nanites deconstructed her into atoms and they left the same way he got in.'

Something was bothering Jen. 'Kirby said NanoMite left them behind, in the War Room?'

'That's what he said.'

'Then that suggests NanoMite was there, at the Foundation. Kirby should know who he is?'

That hadn't occurred to Toby. His mind was still fluffy from lack of sleep. 'Then why would he send us out to find out who NanoMite is?'

Jen looked grave. 'I don't know, but I don't like it.' Then she noticed something on the wall behind Toby. 'What's that?'

It looked as if dust had streaked across the otherwise clean white walls. Toby stared at it, then looked towards the fridge space, then at his own feet as he tried to imagine the villain appearing in the kitchen.

'She was standing right here. The fridge was there. He came out, grabbed her . . . maybe he fired something at her, which means this is residue from that.'

Jen examined the dust closely. 'It's not residue, it's more like . . . graffiti.'

Toby joined her. Against the light grey dust, heavier particles had burnt the wallpaper, leaving a very faint string of characters that repeated themselves:

**68 65 6c 70 20 6d 65 . . . . 1142 SMITH STREET . . . .
68 65 6c 70 20 6d 65**

'That's NanoMite for sure. This string of junk is the same as on the message he left at the Foundation. But why leave an address?' He took a picture of it on his phone.

'So we can forward his mail?' said Jen drily. 'And

The Hunt Begins

there could be hundreds of similar addresses all around the world. Are we going to search them all?'

'Well, he left it for a reason.'

'Yeah, a trap. Just waiting for somebody dumb enough to walk right into it. If she was deconstructed as you said, then he could probably put her back together on the other side? So she's not dead? Those others, those people, they can still be alive?'

'I don't see why not. The question is: what does he need them for?'

NanoMite sensed his defeat in Las Vegas as soon as his nano-Swarm broke communication. He stalked across the cavernous chamber he was using as a lair.

His entire body was held together by nanites, some slightly larger than an atom. The humanoid shape of his body was only something that manifested from a vague memory, although he was sure his knees were not supposed to bend *that* way. That's what gave him his peculiar bobbing gait; not that he was concerned with image.

He had vague memories of what it was like to be human, but since the experiments, he could only remember snatches. They were pictures in his mind. The only emotions he associated with them were hate and rage.

Forty people stood motionless in the room, all snatched so he could use their peculiar talents. Nanites had seeped inside them, through their mouths, noses, ears and even the pores in their skin. The ultra-small machines had tapped into nerve endings and secured even more metal plates and monitoring panels to their bodies, turning them into one single bio-processor. Rather than work within the limits placed by standard silicon processors, NanoMite had developed the ultimate neural network—a computer system running on the brains of the exceptionally intelligent people he had kidnapped. Between them, they were capable of processing calculations millions of times more swiftly than the fastest supercomputer.

They were the backbone of his operation. Through his ingenious living computer network he could process the billions of commands needed to control the swarm anywhere in the world.

He had chosen the victims for their skills in decrypting complex security algorithms and their ability to rapidly program new codes in their heads so that his Swarm could adapt and react to the new challenges it was facing.

The loss of his nanites in Vegas was a small setback. Although they represented only a tiny portion of the micro-machines at his command, he could ill afford to lose any until he could find a way to replicate them.

The Hunt Begins

NanoMite's black eyes scanned his captives. They were still alive. That was progress. The previous batch had died of hunger. He crossed over to a thick set of electrical cables that ran across the circular chamber. The cables were still connected to the electricity grid and provided a convenient access point to the world.

A voice suddenly whispered in his head; it was like a distant echo, a consciousness that argued with him. Sometimes the voice hurt, like needles in the brain. NanoMite roared with frustration and pounded his own head with such force it crunched out of shape. Seconds later the nanobots repaired his skull and the voice had gone. He was relieved. Being a world domineering mega-villain was pressure enough without part of your own subconscious rebelling against you.

NanoMite pushed his fingers into the plastic coated power cable. He didn't damage it as the nanites wove his atoms between the atoms in the wires. It was as if he had passed his hand through water. Once inside he discharged a thousand nanobots. That would be enough for the task. His neural-processors had gathered enough information from the initial attack on Vegas so that the remaining nanites could learn from previous mistakes. They couldn't be stopped the same way twice.

The minuscule machines flowed with the electrons, their Swarm mind navigating them along the power grids, towards the target.

The fire crews and police cars pushed through the excited crowds on Vegas Boulevard. People were babbling about giants and flying people. The police were baffled because the replica Eiffel Tower had vanished, along with half the casino—but there was no trace of wreckage.

Before they could investigate the scene further, the power suddenly blacked out. Blocks in every direction plunged into darkness. The famous strip was engulfed by the night.

The crowd grew restless so the police cars put their spotlights on and a circling police helicopter shone its searchlight down to provide illumination.

Then the police car lights suddenly cut out. The fire trucks ground to a sudden halt as all power was drained from their engines and the police chopper suddenly went silent and plummeted from the sky as it lost all power to the engines.

Cries of panic spread across the crowd as they discovered that their mobile phones, MP3 players, and watches were suddenly powerless.

The machines had begun to revolt.

The Hunt Begins

* * *

Emily looked around the old Spanish fort. It wasn't quite what she had been expecting. The sun beat down from a clear blue Mediterranean sky, raising ghostly heat ripples at the top of the battlements.

Her escort didn't follow her into the main quad, and she noticed more Forge members standing in the shadows, guarding their leader. If the atmosphere hadn't been so tense, she would have laughed at the notion of the Pete she knew leading a group of rebel supers.

Pete stood on the battlements, looking down on her. She gracefully leapt up in a power-assisted jump and smiled broadly at her old friend. Pete watched her carefully, and saw a flicker of repulsion cross her face. It only lasted a fraction of a second, but it was enough.

'You don't like the way I look? I don't blame you.'

'No, no, it's fine,' said Emily hastily. 'You don't look . . . ' she faltered. She couldn't say he looked fine because that would be an obvious lie. Pete's skin was tinted cyan and heavily cracked like old leather. It itched like mad, but he had to be careful scratching it as pieces occasionally fell off. He looked more like the living dead. He self-consciously touched his face.

'I know what I look like, Em. That's why I came out here, to try and get a tan.'

Emily didn't know whether he was joking or not.

'It's good to see you, Pete. Is this yours?' She gestured to the fort.

'Do you mean: did I steal it?' Emily blushed, but refused to look away as Pete stared at her. 'We had a base. It was really cool, in the mountains. You would have loved it,' he said with a sudden spurt of old-Pete enthusiasm. 'But then some idiots from the COE found us and wrecked the place. That's why we took all those precautions before you could come here. We wanted to make sure you were not being followed.'

Emily gazed out at the deep blue sea and picturesque bay. She became embarrassed when she realized that Pete was watching her.

'Why are you here?' he asked. 'I'm guessing that it's not to join Forge?'

'No. Come on, Pete, Forge? What's the point?'

'The point is that we can do what we want. We're not stuck to boring rules! Both the Council and Foundation manipulate people, with us, it's WYSIWYG.'

'*Wizzy-wig?*'

'What you see is what you get,' he said with a smile.

'Pete, you belong with us. Your friends miss you.'

His smile dropped fluidly. 'Friends? Like Toby? He's just like every other bully who used to pick on me. But now . . . now they can't. I'm too powerful.'

The Hunt Begins

'You're wrong about him. And what about friends like Lorna and me?'

Pete refused to meet her gaze. He stared out across the ocean. 'I can't, Em. Kirby would probably try to kill me; after all, I nearly killed him when I escaped from the Foundation hospital.'

'But that was an accident. You weren't in control—Jake Hunter was using you. Kirby knows that.'

Pete gently shook his head. 'There's no going back there, Em. And the Council . . . they're a bunch of losers too. Did you know Jake has poisoned me?' The shocked look on her face clearly indicated that she hadn't heard. 'He placed an artificial virus into my body. A real one, not a computer one.' He thought it best not to mention that Jake had poisoned him in retaliation for Pete almost killing his parents. The truth sounded less sympathetic.

Emily was horrified. 'You can't let him do that to you! We can stop him.'

Pete snorted. 'No one can. Why do you think Forge has been doing all these . . . really bad things lately?'

'Because of Jake?'

'He's set the virus off already, Em. It's eating me from the inside out. The only hope I've got is to interfere with Hunter's mission. Get whatever he needs and use it to convince him to give me the cure!'

Emily felt suddenly angry. She knew Lorna was trying to talk Jake out of his misguided ways. A surge of confidence went through her.

'We'll put a stop to that. Together. We can convince him, Pete. I know we can.'

An expression of hope crossed Pete's face. He wanted to believe her. He wanted to believe there was a way out of the curse he had brought on himself because of hundreds of small, random chances that had pushed his life down this path.

'Do you really think so? I'd resigned myself to thinking that life just had it in for me. Like I was supposed to be a hulking great monster with bad skin.'

Emily smiled. 'I don't believe in destiny. I believe people can change.'

They were unaware of movement on the fortress wall across from them. If anybody had chosen that moment to look then they would have seen the sunlight glint off a small metal chassis. It looked as if a smashed mobile phone had suddenly grown legs and was stalking them. The nanobot raised its scorpion-like tail—but it wasn't tipped with a stinger, instead it had a small satellite dish that it pointed skyward to broadcast the conversation into space.

From his den, thousands of miles away, NanoMite

The Hunt Begins

watched and listened to the conversation. It wasn't displayed on a screen, but instead it was transmitted directly into his brain—a floating image as substantial as a daydream.

'Perfect,' he cackled to himself, his voice echoing around the bare concrete walls. He watched as his kidnapped victims swayed as they processed dynamic chaos theory equations. Even with their blistering speeds, it was still a slow process. He could only increase the speed by recruiting more unwilling volunteers, but he was quickly running out of nanobots. His Machiavellian plan lay at the tipping point—he needed a way to replicate the nanobots before he stretched himself too thin and his scheme failed.

However, his chaos computations had led him towards Pete in a seemingly random, holistic trail. He had a problem and the laws of chaos theory had pointed him towards the solution.

It appeared that Pete Kendall was the answer to his problems.

Jen had wanted to return immediately to the Foundation Headquarters with their latest discovery, but Toby had other thoughts on his mind. He was concerned that Lorna had stolen his phone and disappeared off to do who-knew-what—and she wasn't answering. Last time she had gone missing, she had landed in a world of trouble with Jake Hunter.

He took a deep breath. She was probably with Emily, and at least Emily had the good sense not to get into trouble. If he tried hard enough, he could almost convince himself not to worry.

Toby decided they should head back home to search for his own phone. Following Chameleon's warning, and the fact he didn't want to land his sister in any more trouble, he didn't want to admit to Jen that he'd lost it, so he made the pretext of wanting to talk to Lorna.

They appeared in his bedroom, which was messier than it had ever been. Toby hadn't been around much to tidy it.

'Wait here,' he told Jen and dashed to the door, cautiously peering out in case anybody had heard them arrive. Luckily his parents were out working.

'Wow, is this your room? It's a real dump!'

Toby instantly regretted bringing her back, but it was too late to worry about that now. He bounded down the stairs and checked every room. There was nobody at home. He returned to find Jen sitting with her boots on his desk, reading a comic she'd taken from a stack.

'You still read comics?' There was a note of scorn in her voice.

Toby didn't think it would help to explain that most

of them were Pete's that he had brought round when they had first discovered their powers. Besides, she was reading a new one, so she probably wouldn't believe him. Instead he snatched it from her hands.

'Hey! I was reading that!'

'I thought you didn't like comics?'

'I didn't say that,' she replied defensively. 'Are you hoping to star in one of your own?' There was no avoiding the sarcasm.

'You know, I used to think you were cool.'

'When I was always beating you up?' she said, climbing from the chair.

'I think you'll recall that I outsmarted you pretty much every time.' He didn't like the look that was crossing her face, so he quickly changed the conversation. 'Nobody's at home. I should try calling her.'

He dialled his own phone number. It went straight to voicemail. Toby wanted to kick himself: he was using Kirby's phone. Perhaps Lorna had seen the name flash up and immediately cut the call?

'Is she avoiding your calls?' asked Jen.

'Looks like it.' He tried Emily's mobile and got the same response.

Jen watched him drop onto his bed with a defeated sigh. She felt a sudden pang of sympathy for him, but didn't know why.

'Don't worry about it, shrimp. I'm sure they're fine;

if they were in any trouble the Foundation would know about it.' She gently kicked his feet and smiled. 'Come on, we've got a job to do. We can run that address through to the Foundation and ask them to trace it. In the meantime I'm gonna head home and catch up with my sleep. See ya later.' With a dull thump, she teleported away.

Toby sat on his bed, exhaustion catching up with him. Maybe it was because he was worried about his sister and was so tired that he felt over-emotional and unappreciated. For a fleeting second he wished things could return to the way they were. From the moment he'd got the powers, things had started to go wrong. First with his mother being kidnapped by the overly theatrical Doc Tempest, his home destroyed, then his friendships started to crack shortly after.

A thought suddenly struck him: maybe it was time to retire from the hero business? Hang up the old cape, so to speak, now that he had been consigned to menial jobs?

Or maybe it was time to put the past aside and start thinking about himself? He kicked off his trainers and lay on the bed. He was asleep in seconds.

He hadn't noticed the faint ashen footprint he had trod into his carpet. It was something he had picked up on the sole of his shoes at the crime scene. The dust suddenly moved, betraying its synthetic nature. The nanites clumped together to form a small beetle-shaped silver nanobot that scuttled towards the power socket.

Eric Kirby stared at the huge monitor screen depicting the world's trouble spots. Things were getting worse—worse than usual—and that was saying something. He was feeling intensely guilty about that, as most of it was his own fault.

He looked around the empty control centre. He had ordered everybody out so he could have some time on his own. He'd miss the Foundation when he was gone . . . which he suspected would be sooner than he would have liked. The Foundation had been part of his life for longer than he cared to remember. It had all started over a century ago when he and his brother had discovered an island run by a pirate. That villain had gone on to become his arch-rival and had been equally responsible as Kirby for shaping the world.

A message flashed on the screen for his attention. With a wave of his hand he accessed the 3D interface and deleted the message, unread. He knew what it was. Reaching into his jacket pocket, he pulled out a crumpled map. Scrawled on it were coordinates written by Toby in a hurry—the location of the Council of Evil's ultra-secret headquarters. Toby had risked his life to get this information and had started a crusade to topple the Council. Kirby had done all he could to stall him, but he knew that wasn't enough.

He crumpled the map and threw it into a bin. The bins were enclosed units that microwaved the trash, hygienically incinerating it.

'Sorry . . . ' he murmured.

Another message flashed on the screen. It was a duplicate of the one he had deleted that demanded he attend a meeting. He erased it again. It was time to face the Inner Circle. He absently toyed with the pendant around his neck and headed for a rendezvous that could possibly be his last.

Toby awoke with a start and looked around in momentary confusion. It was dark outside; he must have slept all day. His alarm clock wasn't functioning so he had no idea what time it was. He groped in the dark for his mobile. That was off too. He thumbed the button, but it wouldn't switch on. The battery must be dead.

Slivers of light from a plump moon filtered in through the window, giving him enough illumination to find the light switch. It didn't come on. Toby frowned, why was the power off?

He felt his way along the hallway and into his parents' room. There was nobody there—they hadn't come home yet. He started feeling a surge of panic—what had happened?

He felt his way down the stairs, carefully walking sideways, clinging to the banister to secure his balance. The power was off down here too. He opened the front door and stepped out.

The streetlights were out and there wasn't a single light in any of the houses. With a growing sense of panic he darted back inside and tried the phone line. That was dead too. Now he knew something was wrong and felt the icy claw of panic; his family was missing and the entire town was experiencing a power outage. Toby had seen too many weird things to believe in coincidences. He suspected this was connected to NanoMite.

Out of instinct, he tried to boot up the computer, just in case some weird quirk of fate would power it. Of course, it was dead. As quickly as he dared, he headed back upstairs to grab his dead mobile and trainers, and then headed out to search the streets.

It was eerily still and the cold light from the moon gave the landscape a strange appearance. A yapping dog was soon joined by another in the distance, but the usual ambient noise was conspicuously absent.

It was only after wandering through several empty streets that he realized that not a single car had passed him by. Toby shivered, not from the cold, but from the sudden thought that he was now just an ordinary kid with no powers, and no chance to access Hero.com.

He was on his own.

He became aware of a noise, a constant pittering like hailstones falling on a tin roof. He traced the direction of the sound down two streets; he was now heading towards the high street. He turned a corner—then quickly retreated behind the wall of Mr Patel's newsagent's. He cautiously peered around the side of the building to confirm what he had seen.

Dozens of small nanobots were assembling from parts stolen from an electrical shop. One construct was the size of a coffee table, built, as far as he could ascertain, from the interior drum of a washing machine and sections of a vacuum cleaner that formed thin spider-like legs. Across the street, a car showroom was similarly being looted. The creation there was being assembled from engine parts and had smooth red armoured panels cannibalized from a Lotus sports car. Although he couldn't see them, he knew the disparate components were held together by the nanites. They had clearly followed him home.

What had worried him were the four figures he had seen standing next to the creatures, as if on guard. They were people; in fact he was sure that one of them was Mr Patel. What frightened him was their vacant expressions and the shiny silver components that had bonded into their heads. One woman had a mobile phone seemingly grafted to her skin. The case had been stripped away, revealing the components beneath.

He wasn't sure how, but he was certain the nanites had fused the tech to the people and were controlling them like synthesized humans. It made sense as it dawned on him that, perhaps, the missing people had been specifically chosen for their unique skills to help the nanites and been turned into Synths. He'd have to investigate that further if he managed to get back to the Foundation alive.

He pressed himself flat against the wall in case Mr Patel turned round. Toby held his breath and hoped he hadn't been seen. He was more than aware that he had no powers, no chance of getting any and no way of calling for help.

A rhythmic tapping noise suddenly got his attention, a clinking sound like metallic legs walking across stone. It was coming from above him.

He craned his neck—a nanobot was scuttling vertically down the wall, straight for him. In the moonlight he caught glimpses of tubes, components, and gadgetry that had possibly walked right out of a microwave and a TV.

What he did instantly recognize were the articulated arms barbed with spinning blender blades that had morphed and transformed into wicked knives—which thrust towards his face.

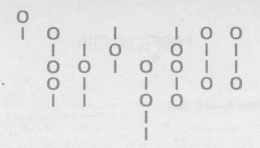

The Inner Circle

The Inner Circle never met in the same place twice. The Circle members themselves were the only ones who knew each other's identities. Even the assistants who accompanied them never got to meet the other members or even their own counterparts.

This session had been scheduled in Antarctica, in a half-demolished ice cavern. Kirby climbed from his private jet, which had landed on a runway that was only approachable via a cave mouth, and ran through two conjoined peaks before ending in the battle-scorched cave.

He lingered briefly to look at the mound of ice that had collapsed during the battle. Under it lay a super-villain called Doc Tempest. He had been Toby's first major victory. Charred detritus had been swept into a pile, but the scorch marks along the walls and ceiling remained witness to the devastating explosion that had torn the hangar apart.

Kirby pulled his thick thermal coat tight and walked through a buckled doorway and down a cold corridor jerry-rigged with lights for the conference. The lights led him on, past dark side tunnels and abandoned rooms. He didn't fear attack, as Circle meetings were always neutral, differences had to be put aside.

The corridor opened into a grand control room ... or it would have been if the instruments and control panels hadn't been blown to smithereens. A temporary table had been erected in the centre of the room, around which sat the Inner Circle. Only three chairs remained vacant—one was Kirby's, one was for Forge, and the other had remained empty for some time.

Kirby nodded to the Circle members and silently took a seat.

'I received your constant messages,' said Kirby drily.

Nobody responded. They were all grave; the world situation was more serious than usual.

Kirby gratefully accepted a hot pot of tea from the table and poured himself a cup. Unfortunately the table jolted on the uneven floor and the hot liquid spilled into the lap of the imposing figure next to him.

'Argh! Bloody hell, you fool!' howled the plangent voice of Necros. 'You've just scalded my groin!'

Kirby quickly apologized and offered the leader of the Council of Evil a napkin to mop the mess up.

Toby sprang away from the wall as a whirling blade

tore chunks of brickwork close to his head. The construct leapt from the wall, landing awkwardly on the pavement. For a moment, Toby thought the impact was going to jolt the machine apart as it had done in Vegas, but it held together. The nanites had learnt not to build large, ungainly nanobots.

The noise had attracted the attention of the other two nanobots and the four Synthed humans. Mr Patel's gaze bore into Toby. It was not a friendly one any more and there was no hint of recognition.

Toby spun on his heels and ran—there was nothing else he could do. A quick glance behind him revealed they were all after him. The machines were far quicker than the humans, which meant they were catching up.

A serrated metal whip lashed out from the blade-whirling mech. It narrowly missed Toby's foot, shattering concrete. He angled away down a dark side street as the whip cracked close to his ear, nicking it and drawing blood. It was only a tiny wound but the pain was unbearable. He zigzagged again in a futile attempt to lose his pursuers.

The street was too dark to make anything out but the silhouettes of buildings against the night sky. Ahead was a bridge that cut across the dark waters of a river. Perhaps he could lose them there.

Toby changed direction again and aimed for the bridge—unfortunately the streets were too dark to see what was underfoot. He became entangled in a full bin bag and fell. The bag ripped open, spewing rotten contents across the road, as Toby slammed into the tarmac, rolling out of control into the side of a car. The impact was so hard he dented the door and would have triggered the car alarm had the electronics been functioning.

The fall was exactly the chance the machines needed. Blade was on him first. Toby savagely kicked the arms aside. The whirling knife slashed his jeans, cutting into his calf. He grunted with pain, but was too focused on surviving to let it distract him.

The car rocked as another nanobot leapt on it. Toby suddenly felt an ice-cold hand clutch his skull tightly. It was a colander-like probe extending from the robot above him. He couldn't move his head, but his eyes frantically rolled in his sockets as he felt the tingle of nanites trickling from the probe and down his temples. He knew once the nanobots had found their way into his brain he would become a mindless Synth like Patel and the others.

His thrashing legs were suddenly pulled tight as the blade nanobot stopped attacking him and aided its buddy in restraining him. Blade crawled on top of Toby, pinning him down. Its forward claws moved to restrain Toby's arms as he tried to punch his way free. He tried to bellow his defiance, but tasted bitter metal as the nanites flew into his mouth. He was completely over-powered.

Then Toby saw a bright flash and heard an incredibly loud bang. All he could see was an after-image of the flash. The explosion had rendered him temporarily deaf. The weight shifted off his chest and his arms were suddenly freed. He frantically wiped his face, shoving the nanobots off that clung to him like grains of sand.

Then he heard a voice. It was muffled and distorted as if it was coming from underwater. 'Are you all right?'

'I can't see!' shouted Toby, probably at the top of his lungs because he was having trouble hearing his own voice. A hand grabbed his arm and pulled him side-ways. He staggered; with his hearing gone his balance was also suffering. He heard a few deep rumbles and felt waves of heat shoot across his face. His hearing and vision started to return—and he looked straight into the smiling face of Jurgen.

'Ah! You are back with us, *ja*!'

'*Ja*,' replied Toby, still a little disorientated. 'How did you find me?'

'That was easy, bro,' said Hayden who was hovering several metres up. He lobbed a fireball, destroying the last of the nano-ensembles with raging flames. 'Lots of places went down, then we heard your town had been hit too. When you didn't report in, Jen traced you through your CUCI.'

Of course, the Cellular Uplink Communication Interface that was inserted into all Downloaders. It relayed vital information about location, health, and power status straight back to the Foundation. The Council of Evil had once replaced his in an elaborate duplicitous scam, but it had been restored once he had escaped. He had thought of using it to find Lorna but Kirby had removed hers once she had been barred from downloading.

'Is Jen here?' He looked around, which was no easy task since he was still feeling dizzy. He saw the four Synths race towards them. 'Watch out!'

Hayden reacted on impulse. He blasted them with a fireball. Toby watched in horror as Mr Patel and the others were thrown off their feet, clothes burning. 'No! What're you doing?'

'Saving your butt! Let's get out of this dump!' said Hayden.

'Mr Patel!' shouted Toby. Hayden suddenly swooped and grabbed his arm. Toby felt dizzy as he was teleported away from his home.

The last thing he saw was his former boss and friend rolling on the floor trying to smother his flaming jacket.

'We all know why we have convened,' said Eric Kirby,

hot vapour puffing from his mouth with each syllable. 'The question is, what are we going to do about it?'

Necros shifted in his seat, doing his best to keep in the shadows and thankful that the room was cold enough to soothe his scalded thigh. 'We? Is it not you who unleashed this latest threat?'

Kirby scowled at his opponent. 'If you are talking about the Dark Hunter, I believe that was a problem one of your minions created.'

'You know very well to whom I refer!' Necros retorted; his doom-laden voice shook loose ice from the ceiling. 'The one who calls himself NanoMite. Already we have had probing attacks made on Council defences. But we have been fortunate enough to repel him. This threatens our Pact, Commander. Some may think this will help Forge. Others think it is time you stepped down.'

Kirby looked away; he was feeling guilty enough without Necros pointing out his failures. 'I am not stepping down, Necros.'

A murmur circled the table. Kirby immediately sensed the tide was against him. A large figure at the end hammered his fist on the table with such force everything shook and risked another tea related attack on Necros. He was known only as the Mediator and both Necros and Kirby respected his opinions.

'That is not for you to decide! That is for us, the

Inner Circle, to vote upon. Necros may be correct in his assertion. But thought must also be given to how you have both brought us to the brink.'

'Me?' declared Necros in surprise. 'I have done nothing but uphold the Pact!'

The Mediator interrupted. 'I wonder if that claim is entirely full of merit. The Pact was established to maintain the status quo, to make sure the planet was not destroyed in all of the madness. Something Mr Grimm and Momentum had visions of achieving, although their methods were too simple and they were not aware we had already taken those steps.'

'Spare the lecture!' moaned Necros.

'I am merely relaying the facts so we can all see who is culpable. Grimm's determination caused the rise of Forge. They think they are in the middle, straddled between good and evil, when in fact they are a self-serving force that is doing harm to both sides. Still, we retain a chair in case they wish to parley with us.' Everybody glanced at the empty seat next to Kirby, reserved for the leader of Forge, should he wish to join the Inner Circle.

'But they don't want to talk,' said Kirby who had been pursuing the matter. 'And I don't see how that relates to NanoMite or the Core Power issue.'

There were six Core Powers; they were the original powers from which every other one had spawned.

The Inner Circle

Only one person at a time could wield a Core Power and they had been deemed too destructive to be used. Recently, a villain called Lord Eon had unleashed his time manipulation on the world. The Core Power inside the pendants was just as devastating as his, and had been locked away and entrusted to Primes to guard. Kirby possessed one pendant, Necros another.

Core Powers were the basis of all superpowers. Lord Eon had run a path of destruction with the Time Core, and now it seemed that Jake Hunter was chasing another Core Power. Nobody wanted him to obtain such strength.

'NanoMite is nothing more than a side problem,' growled Necros. 'Alas, though, it is a problem that affects us all. It appears his ambitions are to synthesize the world into an artificial landscape. He would sooner see us all dead and the machines victorious.'

'I have my people working on that,' retorted Kirby. 'And I have already destroyed the coordinates of the Council headquarters so my people can't attack, as we agreed in the Pact.'

The Mediator spoke up. 'An attack on either head-quarters will be a calamity.' He glanced at Necros. 'Although I recall that you allowed Basilisk to attack the Foundation with a virus, and he very nearly succeeded in destroying it.'

'That was with no help from us!' growled Necros.

'Nevertheless, it was also without hindrance from your side. I think in this instance the Commander has been most gracious in not retaliating with a petty squabble.'

Kirby smiled. It was a small political victory, but he enjoyed winning any points he could over Necros. He tried for another. 'I believe your people were supposed to be dealing with Hunter.'

Necros leaned back in his chair as he suddenly became the focal point of the conversation. He played with a small pendant around his neck, similar to Kirby's.

'He is proving very difficult to crush and, since you bring that up, he is having help from some of your people. A girl. He has two more pendants to collect. Both of which are in this room. He has already started to unlock their power, and we all know that he is too unpredictable to wield a Core Power himself.'

Everybody fell silent at the thought of a teenage boy brandishing something so powerful it could shape the universe.

'What bothers me, is how does Hunter know what to search for?' asked Kirby thoughtfully. 'We erased all records and eliminated all witnesses outside the Circle.'

'Not all,' said Necros. He looked meaningfully at the other empty chair.

Kirby went pale. 'Leech?'

The Inner Circle

'So it would seem,' said the Mediator ominously.

'But why would he do such a thing?'

Necros leaned forward, eager for a chance to needle Kirby. 'Because you locked him away far from his son. He has long desired revenge on you.'

'I entrusted Armageddon into your care,' Kirby spat back. 'It was all I could do to stop him from being killed; it was an act of mercy. Yet you still managed to let Hunter kill him!'

'I looked after your nephew as best I could. Maybe you should have paid more attention to your brother? Perhaps then he wouldn't be helping Hunter destroy us all?'

Silence filled the chamber. Kirby felt turmoil inside. He had tried to do everything for the greater good. Even when his own brother, known as Leech, absorbed a Core Power, he still tried to save him from the execution the Inner Circle had demanded. He had placed Leech far from harm and made sure his twisted evil son was raised by the Council.

Then, when it became apparent Jake Hunter was seeking a Core Power, Kirby had tried to save the world with the creation of NanoMite—and that had backfired too.

How ironic it was that his good and just actions had created more trouble than any of Necros's plans.

The Mediator drummed his fingers on the table.

'That still doesn't resolve what we must do, and what we know must be done. It is time for us all to make sacrifices.'

Kirby bowed his head in shame. His thoughts drifted to Toby . . . so did his regrets.

Jen's eyes were wide with appreciation, and Toby swore he could see her blush.

'Those guys just don't stop being awesome!' she declared as she watched Jurgen and Hayden leave the Foundation control room.

'I think they killed a friend of mine,' protested Toby. 'They teleported me out of there before I could see if he was OK!'

Jen gave him a distasteful look. 'Have some courtesy. They just saved your life!'

Toby opened his mouth to reply, but thought better of it. He was starting to get used to the blind hero worship people had for the twins. He thought it better to change the conversation.

'What has been going on? What happened to my town?'

'It has been overrun by nanobots,' said Jen. 'The same thing happened where I live. We must have picked up some nanites from the apartment we investigated.'

'What about my family?'

'If they weren't home then I guess they broke down somewhere, lots of people have been stranded away from towns and cities. They're safer there,' Jen added reassuringly. 'The nanites spread quickly, short-circuiting everything in their path and then forming swarms to cannibalize machinery they can use to make a larger body.'

Toby nodded. 'Like the one in Vegas. They seem to have already learnt to keep their nanobots small this time, which means they're harder to destroy.'

'You've all read the analysis reports from some heroes on the ground.' She noticed Toby's puzzled expression. 'Don't you read anything you get sent?'

'My phone wasn't working!' He glanced at his mobile; it was switched on. Then he remembered what Kirby had told him. 'The nanites feed on power, including the batteries in these things. Nothing electrical will work around them.'

Jen nodded. 'Exactly. I was lucky that my powers hadn't worn off when they attacked, otherwise I would've been toast. Anyway, the report reckons they have a hive-mind.'

'What's a hive-mind?'

'Each nanite feeds its experiences back to a central processor so they are capable of learning and working things out. There are about a dozen different types of nanites; each does a separate task—deconstruction, navigation, security—lots of different things. Alone they can only do so many tasks, but by sharing those tasks they can work faster and share the result. It also seems that a Swarm here can immediately learn from a Swarm in China. So each time people figure a way of stopping them, like Jurgen's freezing blast, they learn so they can't be stopped again.'

'That sounds awful,' said Toby.

'Yup, it means we can only ever try one way of stopping them. The good news is that NanoMite hasn't figured a way to duplicate the machines yet so they're only attacking sporadically.'

'Where has he hit?' asked Toby.

'Our towns, Vegas, and New York are the big ones but there are smaller pockets all around the world.'

'I don't get what he thinks he'll achieve by knocking out the power and controlling a handful of people in a bunch of unrelated towns?'

Jen shrugged. 'Who knows? Maybe there is no plan? Maybe it's all just random chaos? Anyway, the computer turned up trumps—we got a match on that address we found. It's in Brooklyn.'

Toby hesitated. 'Didn't you say the power was out in New York? We should get back-up. Where's Emily?'

'I haven't heard. Maybe she's with Chameleon because he is AWOL too. Come on, we've got a manhunt to finish and time is against us.'

The Inner Circle

Before Toby could argue, Jen touched him and they teleported away. Yet again, he hadn't had a chance to download any powers.

Smith Street looked just like any other brownstone building in Brooklyn. The streets were dark and deathly quiet when Jen and Toby appeared outside the building.

Toby couldn't help but notice that Jen wasn't as worried as he was about keeping her powers a secret from the public; she didn't care who saw them. However, there was not a soul around or any streetlights on. The sky was paling, signalling an approaching dawn. Toby stifled a yawn despite his long sleep. He couldn't recall teleporting so frequently and was beginning to feel jet-lagged as they instantly crossed time zones. Or should that be tele-lagged?

'This is it,' said Jen pointing to the building number above the door. 'The records showed it was rented to a Philip Epstein.' She walked up the stone steps and tried the door. It was locked.

Toby looked nervously around the street. He couldn't see anybody, but he sensed they were being watched. He looked at his phone, the power was off—at least that was a useful indicator that the nanobots were in the vicinity.

'Are you going to knock?' he asked.

BLAM! Jen booted the door off its hinges. The heavy wooden frame smashed against the hallway wall as it slammed open. She looked quizzically at Toby's shocked expression. 'What? Don't be so uptight!'

'Do you always break and enter buildings rather than just knock?'

'Whenever I can,' she replied sarcastically. 'Like anybody's going to be home.'

She entered. Toby shook his head as he followed; she was more headstrong than he was. Inside was absolutely dark and a quick test of the light switch confirmed the power was off.

Toby closed the front door as best he could; he still couldn't shake the feeling they were being observed. Then they fumbled their way into a living room and sat down in the darkness. There was nothing to do but wait for daylight to come.

Toby woke with a start as Jen shook him.

'Wake up, shrimp. There's enough light.'

Sure enough the sun was up. Toby peered out of the window; the streets were still empty. He hadn't meant to fall asleep, but the lack of rest over the last couple of days had taken its toll.

'How long was I out?'

'An hour, maybe more. I fell asleep too.'

The house was sparsely decorated with old-fashioned

taste. Clearly whoever lived here wasn't concerned with keeping up with trends.

'Nobody's been at home for a while,' commented Toby, running his finger through the thick dust. 'Did the computer find any link to this Epstein and NanoMite?'

'Nothing. I don't quite know what we should be looking for.'

'Anything that doesn't look right.'

It took fifteen minutes to search through all four floors of the apartment.

Jen threw down an H. G. Wells book she had found on the desk. 'There's nothing here! Why would Nano-Mite leave a message that would lead nowhere?'

'Why would he leave a message in the first place,' mused Toby. 'Have you actually looked at any of these?' He was running his finger across the spines of books packing the bookcase. 'They're all on quantum mechanics and nano-technology; well, most of them. There are a few old titles here too.'

'Sounds like this Epstein is the professor Kirby mentioned; the one who became NanoMite. It doesn't explain why he scrawled his address for us.'

Toby spotted a framed diploma on the wall bearing Epstein's name and a string of letters. 'He specialized in nano-technology.'

'So why didn't the Foundation computers flag that up?'

'Perhaps it had been deleted? Kirby did indicate NanoMite had been in the systems.' He frowned and looked around the room. 'There's no computer.'

'Maybe he had a laptop?'

'Perhaps. You would expect a scientist like that to have a computer in his office, right?'

'Now you're definitely taking this detective thing too far. There's no computer, but that's hardly a clue.'

Toby moved across to the dusty desk. 'But there are a lot of pens,' he said examining a pot full of them. 'Which indicates he wasn't using a computer . . . but writing in a journal this big.' He held up his hands to indicate a paperback size.

Jen laughed. 'Wow, amazing. Did you just magic that clue out of the air too?'

'Funny,' said Toby flatly. 'If you look at the desk you can see an imprint in the dust where it used to be.'

Jen was amazed to see he was right. It had been moved a while ago as a thin layer of dust, not quite as thick as the rest, covered the space. She was about to apologize, but Toby was ignoring her—he was scanning the bookshelves again.

'Ah-ha! Got it!' he declared, pulling the correctly sized black journal from the shelf; it had been wedged against a copy of Jonathan Swift's *Gulliver's Travels*. He laid it on the table and opened it. The entries were written in a tiny script, but all in obsessively neat capitals. 'It's talking about technical theories. This is way beyond me.'

The margins were filled with equations and occasional random alphanumeric markings. Toby flicked through and almost immediately came to a page that had been bookmarked with an old photograph. He held the picture up. There were two men shaking hands at an awards ceremony.

'I guess that's Epstein,' said Jen looking at the photo. 'Who is the other guy?'

Toby moved his thumb and they both gasped—it was Eric Kirby.

'So they knew each other?' said Toby.

Jen was incensed. 'He's got us trying to find his friend?'

Something unpleasant was occurring to Toby. 'Kirby said he didn't know him. Why would he lie?'

Jen shrugged. 'The only reason I can think of is if he wants us to do his dirty work for him. I mean, do you blame him? Would you want to kill your friends?'

Toby felt a tremor of anger. Jen suddenly realized what she had said. 'Toby, I'm sorry. I didn't mean anything by that.' She gently touched his arm to calm him. She had been there when Toby had thought he'd killed his best friend Pete. She'd watched Toby break down in tears of remorse. Luckily Pete had survived, but Toby still bore the scars of that initial feeling.

'That's why it makes sense that Kirby wants us to hunt down his friend. He couldn't do it alone.'

'Sometimes I get the feeling that Mr Kirby is not quite the hero he wants us to believe he is,' commented Jen, taking the journal from Toby and flicking through it. 'Look at this!' she exclaimed. Near the front of the journal were notes for an artificially intelligent computer system and a design for the morphing War Room—the same room Toby and Kirby had escaped from in Nevada. 'Epstein created the War Room.'

'That's why Kirby said he'd left something in the system!'

Jen speed-read through the notes. 'The reason the War Room could change shape is because it was constructed by nanites. He refers to it as sandbox construction—each tiny grain works with another to build a solid object.'

Toby paced as he put the clues together. 'So, Epstein worked on nanotechnology that went wrong, and Kirby wants us to stop his old friend.'

'Looks that way.'

'So what went wrong?'

Jen shrugged and flicked through the rest of the journal. 'The last entry says he is going back to the War Room to work on a new project with CC.'

'CC: that's Commander Courage. Does it say what the project is?'

The Inner Circle

'Something about digitization.'

Toby stopped in his tracks. 'We have to go back to the War Room.'

'After what happened to you? Are you crazy?'

'Jen, listen. There is something very wrong here. Kirby is hiding something from us.'

'Now you're getting paranoid.'

'No, and I think NanoMite wants us to find it.'

'Whoa, now you really are jumping to conclusions.'

'He left this address for us at a crime scene! He wanted us to come. He wanted us to find this out.'

'His nanites also wanted you dead. Explain that.'

That was a complicating factor, but Toby was sure there was something else. He could sense a picture forming, but it was as if he was touching it in the dark— he couldn't quite make out the shape of the clues. He took the journal from Jen and flicked to a random page. There were alphanumeric symbols in the margin.

'These are just like the ones we found on both messages NanoMite left behind.'

'That's just junk.'

'What if it's a code?'

Once again, Jen was impressed with his deduction. Further conversation was suddenly cut short by a ferocious roar outside. They crossed to the window.

Below, the street was suddenly full of people. At first Toby thought they were enslaved Synths, but he could see no sign of any tech grafted to their skin. They were ordinary people—and they were chasing a teenager down the street whose arms were laden with food. They easily caught up with him, and the kicking and screaming mob piled onto him.

'It's mob rule out there!' exclaimed Jen. 'They've been without power for twenty-four hours and they've started to act like savages!'

'You have to stop them. Use your powers!'

Jen suddenly looked scared. 'I don't have them any more. They wore off when you were asleep. You?'

'You didn't give me time to download any before we left!'

They turned back to the window, both feeling more frightened than they had done in a long time. Flying supervillains, energy powers, robots, and time controlling archfiends were one thing—but facing a pack of frightened people was another.

Part of NanoMite's diabolical plan was starting to dawn on them. Remove the luxuries and technologies everybody uses as a crutch in their daily lives—power, warmth, instant food, and access to money from cash points—and mankind will fall back to a more primitive way of life and tear each other apart.

As the sun rose, Toby and Jen found themselves stuck in a city whose population numbered almost twenty million—all of them angry and fighting for survival.

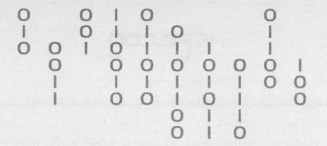

Brooklyn Heights

The meeting with the Inner Circle had adjourned and Kirby made his way back to the jet. He was leaning heavily on his cane, something he had not had to do for some time. Old age was finally catching up with him, and he was far older than he looked, thanks to finding a rare power that slowed down his aging process. His mind was afire with what he had to do. The words of the Inner Circle still rang in his ears. He was being asked to leave behind everything he had helped create, and very nearly destroyed. It had been his life's greatest achievement. And now he had to abandon it.

Not asked, he corrected himself, *told*. Such was the combined power of the Inner Circle, the covert world elite who dabbled in global politics, wars, and industries to keep so many truths from the public.

A rebellious spark nagged at him. He had been ordered to leave the Foundation—but that didn't mean he had to play completely by the rules.

'Kirby!' boomed a voice behind him. Necros was

hunched in the shadows. 'You understand why this must be done?'

Because of a thousand random incidents and mistakes, all running into one another to make the current mess they were in; scientists called it 'chaos theory', thought Kirby, but he found it difficult to speak; the last hour had been emotionally draining. He cleared his throat. 'We all make mistakes, Necros.'

'Indeed we do. *All* of which must be addressed.'

'Meaning?'

'Do not forget your promise to the Inner Circle that you will prevent the Wilkinson boy from attacking my Council. He still knows the location. He is still alive.'

'I will deal with that before the end.'

'Like you did with Hunter's family?' Kirby winced at the reminder. He had used a now deceased superhero called Psych to wipe Jake Hunter's parents' memories of their son. It had seemed a solid, practical idea at the time, but it had resulted in more mayhem than he could have imagined. All of which had helped lead to his unceremonious dismissal.

Kirby looked away, he was sure Necros was taking great delight in taunting him. Eventually Kirby bowed his head. 'As I said, I will deal with it.'

Necros made a rumbling noise in his throat, a guttural acceptance of the agreement. 'It has been an honour battling you, Kirby. Master tacticians like us must always have respect for our enemy.'

Kirby was surprised by the compliment, but wasn't feeling magnanimous enough to return it. Instead, he gave a curt nod of agreement. They would never see one another again in this lifetime; nothing else needed to be said.

Kirby climbed aboard the jet, his conscience heavy. What he did know was he couldn't let the Core Power fall into the wrong hands, and he had to cover his tracks so he could preserve the Foundation.

They were the only two things that mattered to him any more.

'They can't all be under NanoMite's control,' said Toby as the mob outside started torching buildings around them.

Jen was thoughtful. 'I don't think they are. Unfortunately we're looking at good ol' fashioned human behaviour. These people have had no electricity for twenty-fours hours, they're starting to lose it.'

'That's not enough time to go bonkers.'

'Are you kidding? Imagine a whole day without TV, phones, or the Internet!'

She pointed at the lead thug. He was a bull of a man. Heavy muscles were turning into rings of fat around his chin and waist. He was bald, sporting a tattoo of a cobra on the side of his head. His biking leathers added to the Hell's Angel vibe. The dawn light glinted off a metal plate implanted in his skull. 'Cobra there, he's the ringleader. He looks like he's under 'Mite's control. Maybe he is NanoMite?'

'That's not Professor Epstein.'

'He could be dead. You've seen the nanites Synth people. They could have left Epstein's body and gone into Cobra. Look at the way he's leading them. All it takes is one crazy to spark the others off. They've had no communication with the outside world for a day, as far as they know the outside world could have come to an end.' The scope of NanoMite's activities sent a chill down her spine. 'They have no access to ATMs . . . then again credit cards are now worthless. Any frozen or chilled food will start going off and there's no electricity to cook. These people have suddenly been plunged back to living in the Middle Ages, but without the skills to survive it.'

Cobra suddenly looked up and pointed at them. They couldn't hear what he said over the roar of the crowd, but their intentions were clear. As one, the mob swarmed towards the building. Toby heard the front door bang open, and because Jen had smashed the lock, it provided no resistance at all. Feet thundered up the staircase.

Brooklyn Heights

Toby shoved Professor Epstein's journal into his jacket pocket. 'We have to get out of here.'

Jen was pale, panic reflecting in her eyes. 'How? Neither of us have powers.' She banged her mobile phone against the table just in case that reactivated it. It didn't.

Toby knew that attack powers were pointless, he couldn't bring himself to blast a crowd of non-supers. He opened the sash window. Luck was with them: it led straight onto a metal fire escape.

'This way!'

They scrambled out, the rusty metal frame groaning under their weight. A glance below revealed that some of the mob, unable to ascend the main staircase, had had the same idea and were climbing up the fire escape with evil looking expressions and a variety of weapons to hand. The pale-faced guy leading the pack had a knife clamped between his teeth like a pirate.

'Up!' Jen urged.

They scrambled up, the fire escape shaking with every step. Toby gasped, convinced the fire escape was going to pull away from the wall—but it held. It led to the flat roof. Air conditioning blocks and narrow chimneys lay in every direction.

'Now what?' said Toby.

'Now we run!' Jen sped off towards one end of the

block, dodging piping conduits and chimneys. Toby kept close behind her.

A maintenance hatch smashed off fifty metres away. Cobra had punched it from its hinges. He climbed onto the roof, his eyes locked on the fleeing teenagers.

More of the mob made their way to the roof—but Cobra was fast, unusually fast. He easily jumped a metre to clear an air-conditioner unit, just like an Olympic hurdler. He never broke his stride as he vaulted over more pipes and covered cables. Toby knew the nanites must be assisting him, creating bionic parts within his body as he needed them.

'Jen! We've got a big ugly problem behind!'

'We've got an even bigger one ahead!'

They had run out of rooftop. Jen cursed loudly—an entire street prevented access to the next block.

'Toby! What do we do?' There was real panic in her voice, something that Toby had never heard before.

There was another fire escape next to them, but Toby knew that they wouldn't make it halfway down before Cobra caught them. A desperate idea suddenly formed.

'Jen—grab my hand! We're going to run and jump.'

She recoiled from his grasp. 'Are you nuts?'

'Trust me!'

He saw her flicker of doubt replaced by blind trust.

She grabbed his hand. 'I hope you know what you are doing.'

'Me too,' he mumbled as they sprinted towards the fire escape.

They ran as fast as they could—then leapt down onto the steel fire escape. The entire structure rang out from the impact and wobbled violently. Jen and Toby rolled hard, bashing into the thin steel rail that circled each level of the emergency stairs. Their momentum reverberated through the structure again—aging steel pins yanked away from the masonry.

After seeing what a bad state of repair the other fire escape was in, Toby had gambled that this would be the same. The top section they were on pulled half a metre away from the wall, but some rusty pins still held the lower sections to the building.

'Shove us away!' shouted Toby as he braced himself on the fire escape and used his legs to push against the wall. The moment Jen joined in they could hear rusty steel bolts below shearing away.

The snarling face of Cobra appeared above them, as—

The entire steel staircase toppled away from the building like a felled tree. Toby and Jen gripped the lattice floor as they swung across the street. The snarl on Cobra's face didn't disappear, as if he only had one preprogrammed expression of menace.

The top section smashed into the first-floor ledge of

the building opposite, bringing the structure to a sudden halt and catapulting Jen and Toby through a window and into a living room.

They smashed through an old television set, and onto an ancient sofa, which rocked on its castors but remained upright with the two teenagers sitting on it in shock.

Stinging pain shot through Toby's body and he could feel blood trickle down his face. Several shards of window glass had cut him across his body. Jen was in a similar state. Hero.com automatically downloaded a mild healing power with every session, so they had both become used to not feeling any pain, unless it was excruciating. This pain was merely awful.

'You're bleeding,' they both said in unison as they pointed at one another. Then they laughed, not just from the synchronicity, but also because Toby's plan had worked. They looked across at the rooftop they had left behind. Cobra had gone.

'We've still got to get—' began Jen. She stopped when Cobra suddenly appeared on the rooftop. He was running. He sprang off the edge of the roof.

They watched in astonishment as his arms and legs cycled through the air. He landed on the fallen fire escape that ramped to their floor. The staircase buckled from the impact. Cobra might not possess superpowers, but the nanobots were still able to imbue him with supernatural skills. He scuttled up the structure towards them.

Toby pulled Jen through the empty apartment and out into the building's central staircase. Behind they could hear a crash as Cobra pushed his way through the rest of the broken window.

'I'm certain that's NanoMite!' exclaimed Jen.

Toby didn't want to waste breath correcting her as he bounded down the steps and into the entrance hall, Jen at his heels. They were already out of the building by the time Cobra had left the apartment.

They hastened down the road and ducked into a side street to catch their breath and to stem their cuts using the sleeves of their jackets.

'Why is he so mad at us?' demanded Jen between breaths.

Toby patted the journal in his pocket. 'He wants this. Professor Epstein is NanoMite, and if NanoMite is using the bots to control Cobra-head, he'd know we have it.'

'It still doesn't make sense. Why would NanoMite lead us to his home, only to then try and kill us?'

That was baffling Toby too. A loud roar broke his chain of thought. He peeked around the corner to see Cobra had reunited with his posse. Cobra was looking around, his head tilted slightly upwards as he searched for something. His head roved this way and that . . . before sweeping down and staring directly at Toby.

'Oh boy . . . ' he mumbled. He tugged on Jen's arm and they ran for their lives.

Kirby had once again cleared everybody out of the Foundation control room. He ignored the confused looks from the staff and made sure the door was sealed behind them.

He called up the CUCI tracing program from the central computer. Every single beacon appeared on the world map—every hero who was serving the Foundation. Kirby typed in Toby's and Jen's names. The clusters of flashing red markers vanished—leaving two. He zoomed into the map. Real time spy satellites, high in orbit, followed his commands and relayed the live images. Kirby had the perfect bird's-eye view of Toby and Jen fleeing across Brooklyn Bridge, dodging between cars that had been abandoned by their desperate owners. A large mob was following them.

Kirby typed in a command on the keyboard. It would remotely deactivate their CUCI transmissions. He entered his own user ID as authorization. His finger hovered over the button.

He closed his eyes, a tear forming in the corner.

'Forgive me,' he whispered. Then cut the CUCI

data—effectively removing Jen and Toby from the Foundation grid. Nobody would know they were trapped in New York.

A car exploded just behind Toby. The concussion blast from the twisted yellow taxi knocked him and Jen flat. The burning chassis spiralled through the air and crashed on top of an abandoned delivery van, setting that on fire.

'This is not going well,' shouted Jen over the explosion.

Toby peeked over the bumper of the jeep they were crouching behind. Cobra stood on top of a Mercedes, searching for them. Luckily there were enough abandoned vehicles across the three lanes for them to hide. If they could make it across the central pedestrian divider, they would have a further three lanes of cover. The whole bridge was full. It must have been rush hour when the nanobots robbed the city of power.

Cobra's irate mob stayed some way back. They were frightened of their leader's strange new powers. Some had fled, but others watched, unsure what to do, but hedging their bets to stay on his good side.

Toby was perplexed. Cobra had followed them like a bloodhound, how did he always know where they were? Only luck had kept them one step ahead. Oddly, now Cobra almost had them, he could no longer track them, as if something had been switched off.

'I know you're alive!' Cobra bellowed. 'Give me the journal.'

Toby clutched the book in his pocket. There was obviously something in here NanoMite needed, or didn't want him to see. He must have been sending his henchmen along to collect it when they showed up.

'Any ideas?' whispered Jen.

They were halfway along the Brooklyn Bridge. Toby thought if they could make it to the sheer edifices of the Manhattan skyscrapers then they would find it easier to lose the freak.

'We could jump into the water?' They had seen the forty-one metre drop while they were running. The murky waters of the East River hadn't looked inviting.

Cobra extended his hand. Toby saw the skin glow from within as the nanites worked frantically. A blinding oval of energy shot from his hand and blew up a delivery van. Smouldering doughnuts rained down across the bridge.

'Hey, you!' bellowed a new voice. 'This is our turf you shootin' up.'

Toby, Jen, and Cobra all looked around at the same time. A street hoodlum bravely appeared from behind a car and jumped on the bonnet. Toby blinked in surprise as a hundred other mean-looking thugs stood up.

Brooklyn Heights

They were all wearing the same gang colours. They must have been stalking towards the fight unnoticed.

In any other circumstances, Toby would have feared for his life, convinced he was about to get mugged or beaten to death. Now, in the suddenly lawless city, he welcomed the gang's territorial dispute. It was a chance for escape.

Cobra snarled, but didn't answer.

The hood wasn't intimidated. 'You might have some fancy weapon, man. But so do we.'

In a coordinated click-clack, numerous guns, baseball bats, knives and anything that could deliver a hefty wallop, suddenly appeared in the gang's hands.

'We're going to get caught in the middle of a gang-land fight!' whispered Jen urgently.

'I know! Cool isn't it?'

'What if they think we're on the Cobra's side?'

That hadn't occurred to Toby. Somehow he didn't think the new gang was going to be amiable enough to listen to their explanations.

Cobra waved his hand to beckon his own gang forward. After some trepidation they gathered around Cobra, reasoning that it paid to be on the side with the better weapon.

'This is our side o' the bridge,' said the hood, coolly. Toby couldn't work out if he was brave or just plain stupid. 'Go back the way you come, man.'

Cobra jumped from the bonnet—impossibly far—and landed close to the hood. Once again, the hoodlum wasn't fazed. He spat on the ground.

'Now, that was just dumb.'

Toby didn't see what the signal was, but the gangs suddenly yelled as they charged. Toby and Jen crushed together as the jeep they were hiding against rocked from the dozen thugs leaping over it.

Jen tugged Toby's sleeve. 'We have to go!'

Jen proved to be more agile than Toby as they crawled on all-fours between the vehicles. They could hear gunshots, screams, and the occasional explosion, but they didn't want to waste time by watching the battle.

Toby stopped in his tracks as a pair of ripped black jeans jumped down in his path. He looked up to see a wiry Latino guy in his twenties, his face full of piercings in his lips, cheeks, and eyebrows. He swung a fire axe above his head. The guy roared for all he was worth then brought the axe down.

Toby rolled aside; the blade clanged into the asphalt close to his hand. His assailant quickly swung again and again—each time Toby dodged the lethal blade. The last swing brought the axe down millimetres from his groin. Toby's eyes watered from the near miss—his leg automatically kicked out, booting the madman between the legs. His attacker stumbled backwards, axe still in hand. It only took him a few seconds to recover. He lunged again. Toby saw the axe blade rise—

But before it could fall, a fine line, no more substantial than smoke, struck the tip of the axe. The metal blade suddenly dissolved. The fine sand-like particles drifted back towards Cobra. The microscopic metal bonded with Cobra's skin, making it tinge silver.

The skinny thug was left with just the wooden axe handle. Before he could use that, the nanites-swarm smothered his face and began to pull at the piercings. Toby winced when his assailant's skin puckered as the metal stubs in his face were suddenly attracted to Cobra as if by a giant magnet.

Then, with a sickening crunch, the man's face was torn off! Plucked away by each of his piercings. Toby quickly looked away as the guy dropped to his knees, howling in pain.

The Swarm orbited around Cobra—then focused on Toby.

Toby ran. He vaulted onto the bonnet of a Honda, only just leaping off as Cobra blew it up with another energy bolt.

Toby didn't look back. He charged towards Manhattan, slaloming around the vehicles to provide a difficult target for Cobra. Out of the corner of his eye he could see Jen do the same. They had cleared the main bloody street battle that was still raging behind them.

Cobra bounded forwards several metres then stopped. Toby and Jen risked a glance behind and hesitated when they noticed they were no longer being pursued.

'What's he doing?' said Jen, out of breath.

Cobra stood with both arms raised above him, staring to the sky. A plume of fine nanites leapt from his body, glinting in the morning sun. The Swarm made straight for the four thick steel main cables suspending half of the bridge deck.

'I have a bad feeling about this,' muttered Toby.

The cables began to dissolve the moment the tiny robots touched them. Instead of vanishing, the cables suddenly melted off the bolts connecting them to the bridge and fed into Cobra's hands so it now looked as though his arms stretched all the way to the imposing forty-metre-tall, twin-arched brick tower ahead of them.

Then Cobra began to tug. The stone tower grumbled as the cables strained against their saddles at the top of the tower. Masonry dust trickled off the old structures. Toby marvelled that the nanites must possess great strength in numbers.

'We should run,' said Jen firmly.

'Where to?' said Toby, his eyes fixed on the tower. If it fell there would be nowhere they could hide to avoid being crushed.

Brooklyn Heights

The entire bridge started to tremble—then the tower crashed down towards them!

Both Jen and Toby ducked down as bricks pinged from the steel brace that spanned the road above their heads. A massive block of stone flattened a police car to their left. For the first time since he had discovered Hero.com, Toby was convinced he was going to die.

A section of tower the size of a train carriage plunged straight on top of him . . . Toby opened his tightly clenched eyes. Why hadn't he died?

Hayden stood in front of him with a grin. An energy bubble shimmered around him, encompassing Jen and Toby. A chunk of bridge pressed the bubble from above.

'Bro, why is it I'm always saving you lately?'

'What are you doing here?' exclaimed Toby.

'Training wheels are off, bro. We're full fledged heroes, especially after what happened in Vegas.' Toby bit his lip, now wasn't the time to argue facts. 'We got orders to come check the Big Apple since it had fallen off the radar.'

Jen threw herself at Hayden, hugging him tightly. Toby wasn't terribly happy about that, but kept silent.

'Wow! Chicks love us, dude. Being a hero is awesome!'

'Yeah?' snapped Toby impatiently. 'Then hero us out of this mess.'

'Chill! No problemo.'

Toby caught sudden movement through the bubble—it was Jurgen dive-bombing Cobra at supersonic speed.

'What's he doing?' said Toby.

Jurgen landed straight on top of Cobra with such force that the entire bridge quivered as if caught in an earthquake. The shaking didn't stop, if anything it got worse.

Then the deck dropped away beneath their feet and they plummeted into the river!

Massive sections of masonry bounced off the pulsing energy shield, knocking them around like a rubber ball in a washing machine. Inside the sphere they were bashed side-to-side and into each other.

They bobbed in the water as cars and sections of bridge splashed around them. Now they could see that half the bridge deck sloped from the remaining tower on the Brooklyn side, down into the river. While they had endured the rain of debris during the fall, they were now faced with the prospect of hundreds of cars and irate gang members sliding down the incline towards them.

'Man, this is B. A. D.!' said Hayden.

Toby wanted to slap him for spelling out the word. 'Hayden, you've got to get us out of here.'

'No way, bro. We gotta save the folks in those cars.'

'There's no one in them!'

'What about those guys!' He pointed to a thug who rolled into the water—a limousine rolling after him.

'They're criminals!' snapped Toby—and instantly regretted it as Jen and Hayden stared at him.

'Man, that's cold. Who are you to judge them?' Hayden said. He sounded a little injured that his personal hero was talking like a villain. 'You taught me that.'

With the immediate danger of being crushed gone, Hayden banished the energy orb. Toby splashed into the cold water below. Hayden floated in the air above, his arm around Jen to stop her from falling.

'Ladies first, bro.' He swooped Jen to the safety of the remnants of the Manhattan side of the bridge. Jurgen plucked people off the bridge before rolling cars could crush them. He placed the stunned survivors on the Brooklyn side of the bridge.

The strong current caught Toby. He watched as Hayden soared overhead to get him—then changed direction and plucked a struggling thug from the water.

'I'll come back for ya!'

'Wait!' shouted Toby then choked as a wave of dirty water sloshed into his mouth. He frantically trod water, but the current was strong and he was too weak to fight it. Then the water around him started to froth and bubble violently. Something was rising beneath him.

'Help!' pleaded Toby, but the super-twins were too busy saving the gang members who were murdering one another moments earlier.

Cobra rose from the water in a mass of thrashing metal tentacles salvaged from the bridge cable. Multiple metal limbs sprouted all across his body as the nanites fought against the water. Cobra hollered in pain as the micro-machines twisted and distorted his body in an effort to stop being destroyed by the water.

Angry sparks crackled across Cobra's body as the nanites finally short-circuited. Toby desperately tried to swim away but he was too weak.

Jen noticed the activity in the river, and spotted Toby's predicament. She shouted to Jurgen and Hayden for help—but they were too busy saving people, and hi-fiving each other as they crossed paths.

Jen's head snapped back round as the water around Toby broiled—then exploded like a depth charge. Even the twins paused to look around as the nanobots self-destructed in a fountain of water five metres high.

As debris splashed back down, Jen could see no sign of Toby.

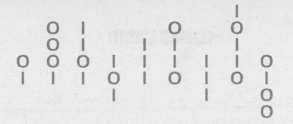

Split Decisions

The first thing Toby saw when he woke up was a fluo-
rescent light. He was in a bland looking room that
could only just pass for a hospital ward. A sense of
déjà-vu hit him. The last time he had woken up in a
hospital room, things had turn out very badly. He was
fully dressed and a quick look in the mirror revealed his
cuts and bruises had vanished, no doubt super-healed
while he had been unconscious.

He left the room and found himself in a familiar
looking corridor. He was in the Foundation headquarters. He felt a little indignant that somebody had
thought his injuries were not substantial enough to
transport him to the Foundation's private hospital,
which was a separate facility. He could have done with
the break.

A muffled cheer came from the end of a long corridor. He cautiously advanced, still not one hundred per
cent sure he was in the correct place. He had been
tricked by the Council of Evil before. They had built a
fake command centre. He followed the noise to the

control room. Now he was closer he could hear dance music. What was going on?

He entered the control room and looked around in bewilderment. The room was full of technicians, a few Primes he recognized, and a bunch of Downloaders. Party streamers popped overhead, dropping multi-coloured paper on his head. Somebody pushed a drink in his hand as they danced past.

Music pounded from the PA system. The centre of the control room had been turned into a dance floor where Jurgen, Hayden, Jen and a dozen others danced. Toby was dumbstruck.

Jurgen saw Toby first. 'Tony!! You are alive! Is good!'

'Thanks,' said Toby, finding his voice. 'What's happening?'

'It's a party, *ja*.'

'So I can see. What for?'

Hayden danced past, hi-fiving Toby—but Toby was too dazed to reciprocate so Hayden's hand narrowly missed slapping him.

'Bro! Victory celebration.'

Toby wondered how long he'd been unconscious, and indeed, if this wasn't still a dream. He was also knotted with jealousy. He had helped save the Foundation from falling apart, he had saved the world—but nobody had ever thrown a party to celebrate those facts. Lorna had always been the one who wanted to be rewarded for their actions; she had dreamed of fame and fortune. Toby had always been morally against that: being a hero was enough for him. Now he was starting to have doubts.

'You've defeated NanoMite?' It was the only reason he could imagine that warranted such a party.

'Nano-who?'

Jen drifted over, a huge grin on her face. 'Toby! You're OK!'

Toby felt dazed. 'I'm alive, thanks for asking,' he replied drily. 'What's happened?'

'This is a celebration party for Jurg and Hayden!'

'What did they do?'

'For starters, they rescued over a hundred people off that bridge when it collapsed.'

'They caused that accident!' exclaimed Toby. 'I watched Jurgen dive-bomb the bridge. That's what made it collapse.'

Jen stopped dancing. Her expression was cold: she obviously didn't agree with him. 'And they killed Nano-Mite. Was that an accident too?'

'Killed him, how?'

'That Cobra guy was NanoMite.'

'No way, Jen. That's impossible.'

Jen crossed her arms and looked stern. 'Why? Because you didn't save the day?'

'No! Because he was way too weak to be NanoMite

and they didn't stop him. The guy short-circuited in the water right in front of me!'

Jen looked smugly at him. 'I thought you said they made the bridge fall. Isn't that how he fell into the river? Besides, as soon as the twins defeated him, all the nanites in New York vanished. Power was restored instantly. They saved thousands more lives from potential starvation and gang fighting.'

Toby was in a state of disbelief. He watched the twins in the centre of the dance floor, surrounded by clapping fans. 'But they didn't do that. What about the missing people?'

'Come on, Toby. Stop being so bitter. It's a few missing people. We'll find them, but NanoMite has gone. Get over yourself. I used to think you were cool, but now it's clear you just want all the attention.'

She turned her back on him and returned to the party, her smile magically reappearing. She avoided further eye contact with Toby.

Toby grabbed the arm of a passing Prime. He was a small man who looked perpetually nervous. Toby couldn't remember his real name, only that he went by the pseudonym of Shudder—and that's about all he could do.

'Where's Kirby?'

'He's not here. I suppose he's out with Chameleon sorting out the moon problem.'

Split Decisions

Toby frowned, *moon problem*?

'Some idiot has put the moon out of orbit. It's heading towards us on a collision course.'

'I need to get in touch with Kirby.'

'No can do. He's incommunicado.'

'Who's in charge?' said Toby with a sinking feeling.

Shudder snatched a drink from a passing tray and slurped it down. Toby realized the Prime was drunk. 'It's a party. Nobody's in charge!'

Toby looked around the room. Was the world going crazy, or was everyone suddenly hero-worshipping Dumb and Dumber? His hand went to the journal still tucked in his jacket. He left the noisy command centre and pulled it out. Some of the pages had stuck together during his dip in the East River, but at least it was dry now.

Jen's comments about NanoMite didn't make sense to him. He needed to verify that the villain was defeated. And even if he was, what was the connection to Eric Kirby and why had Toby been pointed towards the journal?

The first thing Toby did when he left the party was to download several powers now that Kirby's phone was operating. He was tired of being snatched away unprepared. Then he had tried to call home, but the phones were still not working. A quick look on the news revealed that dozens of cities were still without power, including Las Vegas. Any attempt to enter the no-power zones—or NPZs as the media had labelled them—resulted in complete electronic failure. The few reports that came out of the NPZs were bleak—people were rioting and living in fear. Some reporters and rescue workers who entered the zones didn't return.

Toby couldn't understand why the Hero Foundation hadn't moved in to clean these areas up since they were obviously still under the control of the nanites, if not NanoMite himself. But without obvious leadership at the helm of the Foundation, nothing was getting done. Toby hoped his parents were safe. Since they had been missing from the town, he concluded that they were probably safely outside the NPZ. As for Lorna and Emily, he had tried to contact them both on their mobiles, but it went straight to answerphone.

He was on his own. No friends, no family, no support from the Foundation. He felt a twinge of regret that he didn't have Pete to rely on. He quickly pushed those depressing thoughts from his head.

He found a quiet room and read through the journal. Unfortunately the water had run some of the ink, so swathes were unreadable. One passage revealed why the technology-inclined Epstein had resorted to recording his notes with the more traditional pen and ink:

security. In the days of identity theft, computer hacking, and electronic money fraud, Professor Epstein had concluded that paper money and pen and ink were the most secure things in the world.

The readable text in the journal told of a man who appeared to be emotionally torn. One paragraph would highlight the benefits of the nanotechnology he was developing—artificially intelligent machines that could enter a human body and physically destroy cancer. Other paragraphs bemoaned the violent uses to which his creations could be put. Occasionally, Epstein would refer to himself in the third person—Toby only knew he was writing about himself because the handwriting hadn't changed.

Toby was convinced there was something important hidden within the journal. Cobra, under the control of the nanites, had demanded its return. However, if there were any clues hidden in the journal then he couldn't find them, or the water damage had destroyed them for ever.

The only references of note he could find came towards the end of the journal when Epstein exclaimed with delight at the chance to work with his old friend Eric Kirby. Toby guessed this was when the professor had been asked to create the War Room.

If any answers were to be found, it would be back there.

* * *

Pete and Emily pushed through the oven-warm streets of Cairo, past rows of market stall traders who were all noisily advertising their wares to tourists. The pungent smells were overpowering to the senses, some pleasant, some not so much. They had arrived in Egypt because Emily had finally convinced Pete they could plead with Hunter's better nature to cure the virus eating away inside him. They had found Jake . . . but the situation had escalated beyond all expectations.

They stopped at a corner to catch their breath. Fortunately, Pete had reverted back to his normal form; minutes earlier he had been a hulking great monstrosity.

Toby had warned her that a by-product of Pete absorbing so many raw superpowers was that his body now soaked up any impacts—the more you hit him the bigger he grew. It made Pete very difficult to defeat. Despite being pre-warned, the sight of a three metre tall Pete stomping around was frightening. Emily was glad he was back to normal. Or as normal as his crumbling cyan skin allowed him to be.

Pete propped himself up against the wall, ready to throw up. Emily watched with concern. The sickness Jake Hunter had implanted in him was starting to take hold.

Split Decisions

Pete didn't think he had much time left. With the certainty that he was going to die looming ever closer, his outlook on life had changed in the last twenty-four hours. All the criminal activities he had been forced to do with Forge, most under blackmail by Hunter, now seemed pointless—even if Pete and the other members of Forge had enjoyed such wealth and luxuries that had previously been beyond their means.

Now, money was unimportant. What did seem important now was doing the right thing and safeguarding friendships. Reconciliation with Lorna and Toby was something he desperately wanted, but, at the moment, was out of the question, which meant he only had Emily left. He even felt an unexpected desire to find his parents. They had split up months ago and, as far as he knew, had no idea where he was.

'Are you OK?' asked Emily with concern.

Pete was feeling dizzy, but nodded. 'Fine. That fight just took it out of me.' He was feeling sore and bruised from the epic battle that had just taken place. A lot of things had happened, he just wasn't sure exactly *what*, as it had happened too fast. The moment Eric Kirby had shown up, things had got out of hand, especially when . . . he shuddered, it was best not to think about *that*. He blotted those unpleasant things from his mind and focused on what was important—staying alive.

A murmur rose through the market place. The crowd

had become aware of the growing pall of smoke rising from the direction of the pyramids. The cloud blotted out the impossibly large moon that hung in the sky. People began to yell and run towards the smoke to get a better look as they realized it was a major incident.

Pete and Emily hastily walked in the opposite direction.

Emily spoke up after a moment's silence. 'We should get out of here.'

'As soon as our teleport powers recharge,' agreed Pete. His mouth was dry from both his illness and the dry desert heat.

'In that case, let's keep walking. The more distance we can put between that disaster zone and us . . . ' she trailed off. She was still in shock too.

They took a few random turns down roads that were enclosed on both sides by distinctive Cairo sandstone buildings, and crisscrossed above by numerous telephone and power cables. The road they now found themselves on was empty. Packing crates and barrels were piled high against one wall, sitting on which was a gang of five local youths. Two were playing with rusty knives. They stared at Pete and Emily with undisguised menace.

'Terrific,' whispered Emily.

Despite his fatigue, Pete couldn't stop himself from laughing as the gang jumped down to block their path.

Split Decisions

He had once been terrified of bullies, a victim himself. Now he couldn't tolerate them. Both he and Emily had exhausted their teleport powers, and they needed time to recharge. He raised his hand ready to dispatch them with a single superpower, but Emily quickly pushed it down.

'I'm sure we can talk our way out of this,' she whispered, then, in a loud confident voice she smiled at the youths. 'Excuse us.'

The politeness confused the youths who were more used to tourists dropping their possessions and fleeing when they showed their knives. They quickly recovered.

'Your money,' said the leader, holding his blade up for emphasis.

'Not today, thank you,' replied Emily primly and tried to walk past.

The leader's free hand shot out and pushed her back. 'You're not going anywhere.'

Pete rolled his eyes. 'I don't have time for this. Quite literally, I don't have time.' He raised his hand.

The leader was suddenly plucked off his feet and hurled into the crates with such force they were torn into splinters. The other youths looked around in panic. They hadn't seen Pete move so assumed the attack had come from behind them—but there was nobody else there.

Another mugger was lifted off his feet and thrown with such force he sailed over a rooftop, screaming the whole way. The three other muggers stood back-to-back in an attempt to defend themselves.

Emily watched in surprise as the ground beneath them suddenly dropped like the sands of an egg timer. All three thugs were sucked beneath the ground.

Silence reigned once again. Pete was confused as he examined his hand.

'Well . . . that's a new one.'

'I was trying to be diplomatic!' complained Emily. 'What did you do to them?'

'I have no idea!' protested Pete. 'But you've got to admit, it was cool . . . but I don't think it was me.'

Then movement from behind got their attention. They turned to see their saviour—and their eyes widened in astonishment.

The torch cut through the darkness, illuminating chunks of masonry and walls pitted by a variety of high energy impacts. Gravel crunched under Toby's trainers as he descended the stairs that he and Kirby had fled up earlier.

The War Room complex had been evacuated after the Nebulous system had revolted and Foundation employees hadn't returned since. Toby hoped that the nanites had all left when they formed the giant nanobot that had attacked Vegas. At least now he was fully charged with powers if he had to face any that were left behind. The very fact his torch was still illuminated proved that there was no nanite activity around.

He reached the lower levels without incident, although it was spooky to walk around the dark complex alone. He passed through the blast door with the gaping hole in the centre and, at the junction, turned away from the War Room. He was heading to the control room.

The War Room control room had been heavily damaged by fire. It smelt of smoke and melted plastic. Half the computers had had their guts wrenched apart as the nanites had cannibalized them to make the Nebulous vehicles more formidable.

Toby cast his light around the room. There were no clues he could glean from the wreckage. Then a sparking cable caught his attention as it swung from the ceiling. It indicated that power must still be on.

He moved to a terminal furthest from the fire damage and randomly pressed a key on the system. Nothing happened. Frustrated he pounded the desk several times as he had no monitor to take his frustrations out on.

The computer suddenly bleeped and a holographic screen hovered in the air, so bright it temporarily blinded him. As soon as his eyes adjusted to the light, he could see the projection glitch as it hung in the air, and a corner of the holograph was distorted as though the projection lens had been damaged. But it was enough for Toby.

'Access files on Professor Epstein,' said Toby in a firm voice that echoed around the room.

The computer responded with four returns. One was a profile of Epstein who hadn't changed much from the photograph Toby had found in the apartment. Another referenced Project Nebulous. Toby scanned through the jargon-heavy file. As far as he could tell it was the instruction manual on how to use the War Room. Simple diagrams explained how the terrain was constructed from thousands of nanites that could take on any shape and form.

From the journal entries Toby had read, it was clear that Epstein hadn't wanted his creations to be used for war and he wondered how the professor felt about them being used to train for combat.

He was about to close the file with a wave of his hand when a sub-folder caught his eye: 'PSYCHI-ATRIC PROFILE'. Toby was intrigued. He tapped on the holographic folder and it opened a medical document. In this, Epstein looked thinner than in previous pictures. The warm smile had vanished from his face.

Toby speed-read through the text. Several terms

sprang out: HUNGER STRIKE, FORCED REHABILI-TATION and DID. The small text was hurting his eyes.

'Computer, read "Hunger Strike".'

A dispassionate female voice crackled from the remaining speaker.

'Prisoner Epstein refused to eat for three days. Doctors forced nutrition supplements to avoid starvation and mind control hyper-energy protocols to ensure prisoner finished his tasks.'

'Whoa, stop. Prisoner?'

'Professor Epstein was allotted prisoner status two months ago.'

'Why?'

'Refusal to continue work on Project Swift.'

So the Foundation had held Epstein prisoner for refusing to work on a project. Somehow that didn't surprise Toby, which was worrying because it was exactly the type of thing he would expect the Council of Evil to do.

'What is Project Swift?'

'Classified. Password required.'

Toby groaned; he had no idea how to bypass security software. This was more Pete and Emily's territory.

'For the password, try the word "password",' he suggested.

'Incorrect.'

'Nano?'

'Incorrect.'

Toby racked his brain. He offered as many synonyms for 'small' as he could think of: they were all incorrect. He tried to think like a scientist . . . then corrected himself: a *clever* scientist.

'Got it! Try "Lilliput",' he said, referring to the land of tiny people in *Gulliver's Travels*—the very book that was on Epstein's shelf—and written by Jonathan *Swift*. That had to be it!

'Incorrect.'

'What?' he cried incredulously. He tried to remember the story, but it had been so long since he read it. 'What about: Lilliputian?'

'Incorrect.'

Toby swore rather crudely and thumped the control desk.

'Incorrect,' replied the computer referring to his profanity. Toby was sure there was an edge of sarcasm to the voice that time.

He looked back up the list. Epstein had tried to starve himself to death rather than work on the project. He guessed that 'forced rehabilitation' was the use of mind control to get him working again. The other term baffled him.

'What is "did"?'

'I do not understand. Please rephrase the question.'

Toby drummed his fingers impatiently. He thought

the Foundation could have developed a smarter system with all the artificial intelligence software they had developed. What else could 'did' mean?

'OK, what is D.I.D.?'

That did the trick. The screen suddenly changed to another report.

'Professor Philip Epstein's psychological summary. The patient suffered from Disassociative Identity Disorder as a side effect of his work. He developed a second distinct personality after experimentation.'

'A split personality?' Toby had thought that was schizophrenia—obviously he was wrong.

'Correct. The second personality was warlike and aggressive.'

'So that's where NanoMite came from . . . ' he muttered.

'There is a high likelihood that formation of Nano-Mite came from the dominant aggressive personality,' chimed the computer.

Toby needed to know what was in the Project Swift file to make sense of why Kirby had imprisoned the professor.

'Where was Epstein imprisoned?'

'Cell Block B. Lower level.'

'I thought this was the lowest level?'

'Incorrect.' A three-dimensional map suddenly appeared on screen showing Toby the hidden level. It was accessible only through the doorway across from the control room.

Toby cautiously approached the door, wondering what other secrets Kirby had kept from him.

Despite the party atmosphere, Jen was furious with Toby. They had started to make a good team, and he had to go and ruin it all by behaving like a spoilt brat. She knew he was jealous of the twins, and he had a lot to be jealous about—they were good-looking, fun, and had a superb heroic track record already. The ironic thing was that they had been trained to be great supers by Toby. Why didn't he see that as a triumph rather than a hindrance?

She suddenly noticed a message flashing on the screen, unnoticed by the technicians who were crowded around Hayden and Jurgen. The twins were having a dance-off, made all the more spectacular by the use of their superpowers. Hayden was currently spinning on his head, moving so fast that a dent was forming in the tiled floor.

She tried to ignore the flashing screen, but she couldn't. She had always been told her intuition was good, and something about the blinking message screamed 'urgent'.

She crossed over and played the incoming video

message. She only watched the first few seconds before turning to the party crowd and shouting at the top of her lungs for them to shut up.

Something serious had happened.

With the lifts out of action, Toby had to take a short flight of stairs down to the prison level. The Nebulous machines hadn't reached down here, so everything was untouched. A heavy steel door opened with a gentle shove, since all the electronic locks had disengaged when the power was lost.

Toby tensed, aware that any escaped prisoners could still be lurking around. But the four cells were empty. Three of them looked untouched, but the fourth was clearly Epstein's.

There was a single bed with a thin blanket and that was all. There was no table, shelves, or personal belongings. Toby's light played over a stream of symbols on the wall, similar to the ones scrawled through the journal:

42 6c 65 66 75 73 63 75

'Why write the same junk?' wondered Toby under his breath. Even though he was alone, the oppressive atmosphere made him want to whisper. Then something caught his attention: written in smaller script, where Epstein's head would have lain, was a string of numbers—all zeroes and ones. Toby recognized them as binary numbers, the on or off digits that were at the core of computing.

01101001 01110011 00100000 01110100 01101000
01100101 00100000 01110000 01100001 01110011
01110011 01110111 01101111 01110010 01100100

He leaned closer, wondering if they were the mad ramblings of Epstein's second personality. He used his phone to take a picture of the binary code and the rest of the junk. Perhaps greater minds than his could figure it out.

He searched under the bed and between the sheets just in case Epstein had hidden anything, before returning to the control room.

Toby wirelessly sent the picture of the binary code to the computer.

'Can you decipher this?'

The binary digits appeared on the screen then flickered into letters as each was translated.

The computer said, 'The message reads: "Is the password".'

Toby stared at the words hovering on the screen. 'That's it? What does that mean?'

'There is a ninety-five per cent chance that it refers

to the hexadecimal code written on the wall within the image.'

Hexadecimal! Toby almost blurted it aloud. The letters and numbers Kirby had mistaken for junk was hexadecimal code! It was another computer code he had seen used in art packages when referring to colour palettes. He remembered a teacher telling him that it had been designed as a user-friendly version of binary.

'OK, try the hexadecimal code as the password to Project Swift.'

'Incorrect.'

'Are you sure?' It was a stupid question, but Toby was loath to see victory snatched away from him. 'Wait, decode the hexadecimal.'

The alphanumeric figures hovered on the screen, then fell away, every pair revealing a letter: 42 became a capital B; 6C became a lowercase l; 65 became an E . . .

Toby read out the revealed word. '*Blefuscu*? What the hell does that mean?'

'It is a reference to the fictional miniature kingdom that rivalled Lilliput. Password accepted.'

The screen was suddenly awash with files on Project Swift. Toby eagerly digested them. As he read, a picture of split opinions and backstabbing was beginning to form.

Epstein's work on creating nanotechnology to help

cure serious diseases by injecting the machines into humans had hit financial troubles. Eric Kirby had come along and offered to help his old friend. If Epstein created the War Room to train supers in combat situations, then Kirby would ensure the professor had permanent financing for his nano project.

Images of the different nanites appeared on-screen. There were dozens of them, each assigned to do a specific task. A thousand 'security drones' could work together to destroy a cancerous cell, while a 'clean-up bot' would suck up the detritus and recycle it as fuel for the other nanites, or transform the waste matter into a new substance so they could heal wounds or even regrow entire limbs. They formed a perfect miniature factory, capable of doing almost anything.

Epstein had completed the War Room, and in doing so had advanced his nanotechnology, but at a cost to his own mental health. He had become increasingly unstable, switching between his own personality and a corrupt, warlike one that was the antithesis of everything he was.

When he was in this violent mode, his work was superb and Kirby began to see the potential of using the nanotechnology as a true, downloadable weapon. Kirby encouraged Epstein's aggressive personality to create a nano-chamber, a room that would bombard a person with millions of nanites to create a superhuman, no longer reliant on superpowers, but made stronger and faster by the bots fusing with muscles and creating bionic enhancements. The added bonus was that the bots could also utilize Nebulous technology and download powers as required. Theoretically this would prevent the possibility of the power-overload that Pete encountered.

The combined creation would be the ultimate weapon.

Kirby had become obsessed with the concept and pushed Epstein to breaking point. Finally, under pressure, the evil streak superseded Epstein's personality and the monster was born. He killed three Foundation scientists for no apparent reason, and after that was confined to a cell when not working on Project Swift.

Toby was shocked by what he read. It portrayed his old mentor—the man whose life he had saved in the Mexican jungle—as a power-crazed maniac.

Kirby realized the same technology that allowed the nanites to enter a human and kill disease could also be used to strip superpowers out of people. Initial findings revealed that the nanites could destroy the genetic links that made Primes so special—permanently stripping them of their powers. The same principle could be used to suck the powers right out of Jake Hunter and Peter Kendall.

Toby reeled at seeing his friend's name on the screen.

Had his initial assumptions about Kirby been wrong? Had he in fact driven Epstein to madness in order to save Jake and Pete from themselves? Or had Kirby seen the potential to strip the powers out of every super in the world, thus making him the last man standing?

The file concluded with the nano-chamber being created. The Foundation had been furiously at work creating more nanites for the experiment, but the process was slow and difficult.

Kirby had needed to fast-track the experiments once he realized Jake Hunter was looking for the Core Powers. Because of the rush, Epstein volunteered to be the guinea pig for trying the new technology, despite protests from his sane alter ego. Nobody had ever bonded nanites into a human body.

The process of placing Epstein into the chamber and bombarding him with millions of nanites, which seeped into his body, almost tore the man apart . . . but he survived. The nanites must have pushed his madness over the edge because he then attacked the Foundation and allowed the micro-machines to digitize his body into atoms so he could escape through the electrical system.

The nanotech facility was destroyed along with every scrap of data relating to how to create them. Without the plans to duplicate the nanites, NanoMite remained

a limited liability. If he discovered a method of dupli-
cating the nanites at his control, then he would be a
serious world threat.

Toby re-read the end of the file. No wonder Kirby
wanted NanoMite stopped—he had helped create him.
Whether he was doing it for the right or wrong reasons
was irrelevant—the monster had escaped.

Something was nagging Toby. 'Computer, bring up
the message NanoMite left behind for Kirby.'

**74 72 61 70 70 65 64 . . . . . . NANOMITE LIVES!
THE END OF DAYS IS COMING! 74 72 61
70 70 65 64**

'Translate the hexadecimal code.'

'74 72 61 70 70 65 64' suddenly turned into the
word: 'Trapped'.

Toby gasped. He thumbed through his phone and
found the pictures he had taken that had led them to
Smith Street—sure enough the junk that had been at
the start of the message was hexadecimal.

'Translate the code on this,' he said as he wirelessly
transferred the picture.

'68 65 6c 70 20 6d 65' decoded into one simple sentence: 'Help Me'.

Toby stared at the words. Epstein's original personality still survived in the dark recesses of the maniac's

mind and he was calling out for help, leaving clues for somebody to stop the terror he had created!

It was also becoming clearer that Jen was right, Kirby hadn't wanted to kill his friend so had sent Jen and Toby out to do his dirty work. The split personalities explained the contradictory chain of events. The sane personality had left the clue Toby had found, the NanoMite one had controlled Cobra to destroy him.

Another thing was sure, after all he had read: Dumb and Dumber hadn't defeated NanoMite.

The killer was still out there.

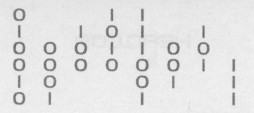

Chaos Effect

Emily and Pete couldn't tear their eyes away from the spectacle in the narrow Cairo street. Nanites poured from the overhead power lines like sand, forming NanoMite from the feet up, as if the machines were being poured into an invisible mould. The villain's wiry body pulsed with points of light that raced across his skin—rough skin that reminded Pete of a circuit board.

They were further surprised when six kids suddenly oozed out of the power lines. Their eyes blank, circuitry grafted to almost every centimetre of their heads. Their hands glowed menacingly red, illuminated from the inside so the bones in their fingers could be seen.

Emily recognized them as the missing children who had flashed up in a Foundation report. She recalled the name of the nearest kid: Trevor.

NanoMite took a step forward, his heavy footfall kicking up a cloud of dust.

'Peter Kendall?' sawed NanoMite's electronically enhanced voice.

'Not me,' replied Pete quickly.

The villain's face looked like a puppet's, a lot of the mobility had vanished. However, he still managed to look mean.

'I am NanoMite. You cannot lie to me. My sensors detect your genetic profile matches the files of Pete Kendall.'

Emily whispered low to Trevor. 'Hey, kid! Your name's Trevor, right? Can you hear me?'

Trevor remained emotionless. NanoMite swung around to look directly at Emily.

'They will not respond to you, Emily Harper. They have been assimilated by my nanites to obey only me.'

'Why have you abducted them? They're only children!' Emily knew she was too weak to face another battle, and her best chances lay in stalling NanoMite until her teleport power had recharged.

'They had trained in the art of combat through video games. Those I selected as my Cohort have more training and faster reflexes than any soldier. The application of my machines has transformed them into unstoppable warriors.' He pointed a gnarled finger at Emily. 'You are expendable.' He swung back to face Pete. 'But I have need of you.'

Emily slowly edged backwards, using Pete as a shield. Pete cracked his knuckles in what he hoped was a menacing manner. It had no effect on his opponents.

Chaos Effect

'What do you want me for?'

'The unique combination and dosage of hyper-energy within your body means that you possess the ability to forge new powers. There is a specific power that only you possess. I require it to replicate my nanite Swarm.'

'Would you believe that's the only power I can't do?'

'Do not lie to me, boy,' growled NanoMite, approaching Pete. The villain smelt like the warm fuzzy electronic odour that came from the back of a warm television or computer. 'I have intensified my search for you. I have temporarily recalled my Swarm from assimilating New York so I could find you.'

'Well, I'm honoured. But I don't think you're the type of business partner I'm interested in. No offence. Come on, Em.'

Pete slowly backed away, pushing Emily with him. NanoMite hadn't been expecting the glib remarks and, as far as they could tell, his face was twisted in confusion.

'You misunderstand, boy. I was not asking.' A cloud rose from his shoulders. For a second, Pete thought it was smoke, but when it swirled like a swarm of tiny bees he realized they were nanites. 'I will extract the powers from your body one molecule at a time. It will be the most painful sensation that you have ever experienced.'

'That's not the best advertisement I've heard for helping you out, so I'll have to say no.'

The nano Swarm shot forward, forming a spear-like column in the air. Pete's experience on Foundation missions and leading Forge had forced him to think one step ahead of his opponents. He formed a power that swelled his lungs—then he exhaled.

The hurricane blast that erupted from Pete's lips effortlessly dispersed the cloud. The six junior Cohorts were plucked off their feet. Two slammed into buildings, the remaining four were blown a hundred metres down the street, rolling head-over-heels and randomly firing energy bolts in every direction. Crates and barrels followed them, splintering apart and spilling their contents as they bounced.

NanoMite bent forward, almost at a thirty-degree angle. Massive steel claws formed in his feet and anchored him to the ground.

Pete stopped the wind blast and spun round, grabbing Emily around the waist as he bounded over the buildings—crashing down on a stall in a parallel street. They sprawled in a pile of dates and splintered wood as the irate stallholder, who was at the end of the street gazing at the smoke from the pyramids, ran towards them.

Emily was first on her feet as a stream of particles arced over the building, glinting in the sun like a rainbow. They quickly formed NanoMite, but Emily and Pete were on their feet and sprinting down the street before the villain was half-formed.

NanoMite sped after them. Rather than run, his feet glided across the floor and he leaned forward like an inline speed skater, crashing through stalls to catch them up.

NanoMite saw them turn a corner, which he reached seconds later. It was another long road, similar to all the others—but there was no sign of Pete and Emily. He hesitated, they couldn't have gone far and he hadn't detected a teleport shockwave.

Emily held her breath, clutching onto Pete's arm. She had turned invisible, and by touching Pete had concentrated on spreading the invisibility to encompass him. They watched as the fiend's head scanned the street, searching for them. He slowly stalked past, forcing Emily to push further back against the car they were hiding behind.

NanoMite suddenly stopped—had he heard them? The villain's head altered shape as nanites scurried over him, building something around his eyes. When he turned his head, Emily could see the bots had created red-tinted filters over his eyes that reminded her of nightvision goggles.

NanoMite turned round . . . further . . . then stopped—staring straight at them. His machines had formed a device that could analyse the entire light spectrum. They may be invisible, but their heat signatures stood out in bright reds and oranges on Nano-Mite's thermal imaging sensors.

'That was a great idea, Em. But I think it's time we left.'

Pete's teleportation power surged through his body and he whisked them both out of the danger zone—just as NanoMite sprayed his nanites over the car, dissolving their hiding place into a pile of component parts.

He howled with fury—his valuable prize had eluded him!

Toby reappeared back at the Foundation headquarters—although he had no idea what he was going to do. His mind was reeling with facts and conflicting opinions over Kirby.

The first thing he had to do was check if NanoMite was truly active, or if the blackouts were simply a lingering side effect. He wanted to avoid the idol worship in the command centre so headed straight for Kirby's private office. If he were to find any more clues it would be there.

Kirby's office was spacious and decorated in oak. Massive windows overlooked the tranquil unnamed forest outside. Toby had no idea where the headquarters were located, he had never travelled here by anything other than superpowers.

He sat in Kirby's luxury chair that contoured around his back, and accessed the computer.

'Search for any signs of NanoMite activity,' he commanded.

The holographic screen threw up a world map with the word 'SEARCHING' emblazoned across it. Seconds later the map zoomed in on one region, most of which was obscured by smoke.

'Nanite activity has been detected in troubles in Cairo, Egypt. There is a ninety-eight percentile probability that NanoMite was involved.'

'Troubles?'

'A battle occurred in this location twelve minutes ago with multiple Foundation participants.'

Names flashed up on the screen—three of which caught his eye: Chameleon, Emily, and Kirby. Toby felt his heart hammering in his chest—had Emily got herself tangled in the NanoMite mess?

'What's the status on Emily Harper?'

'Data from her CUCI indicates her vitals are stable.' The map changed to a different location as the system focused on her CUCI.

Toby was relieved she was safe. 'What about Chameleon?'

'I cannot find any data.'

'What does that mean?'

'I cannot find any data.'

'Is he alive?' he asked with a tremble in his voice.

'Insufficient data available.'

'What about Kirby?'

'I cannot find any data.'

That didn't mean they were dead . . . but it wasn't good news. 'Is this linked with NanoMite?'

'Their CUCI uplink was severed before the appearance of NanoMite.'

'Call Kirby's phone!'

The computer dialled the number—then Toby's phone rang. The sudden noise made him jump from his seat. He pulled the phone out to see it was the Foundation's number—of course! Kirby had given him his phone before he disappeared. An UNREAD MESSAGE icon flashed at the bottom of the screen, no doubt a personal one for Kirby. Toby had more pressing thoughts than to deal with Kirby's inbox. NanoMite was still on the loose and Dumb and Dumber had convinced the Foundation they'd defeated him. He needed somebody to listen to him, to help him convince everybody that the twins had been wrong.

'Is Jen still in the building?'

'I cannot locate her CUCI data.'

'What does that mean?'

'Insufficient—'

'Shut up!' snapped Toby. He was getting tired of the witless machine. Then something occurred to him. 'Can you detect my CUCI data?'

'Negative.'

Toby stared at his wrist where the microscopic transmitter was embedded. Had both his and Jen's stopped working at the same time? Then something awful occurred to him. 'Did NanoMite deactivate our CUCIs? Has he infected us with his nanites?'

'Negative. Your CUCIs were deleted directly from the Foundation while you were both stationed in Brooklyn.'

'Deleted? By who?'

'My records show that the authorization came from Eric Kirby.'

The revelation shocked him. Kirby had deleted the only transmitter that could alert anyone to their peril. The twins had saved them—Toby hated using that expression—in Las Vegas by tracking their CUCI info, but Hayden had only found them on the bridge by chance. Because Kirby had deactivated the CUCI it meant they couldn't be rescued a second time—exactly the time when they had located Professor Epstein's journal with evidence that incriminated Kirby!

That drove Toby towards one inevitable conclusion— Eric Kirby had tried to kill them both!

He sprang from the chair and headed for the Command Centre. The music was still playing as he drew nearer.

The party was still in full swing, although most people now sat down in small groups, animatedly talking. The overriding smell of pizza hit Toby as he entered. A dozen empty pizza boxes were stacked on the floor.

He scanned the crowd and saw Jen talking quietly in the corner with Hayden.

'Jen, I need to speak to you!'

She scowled at the intrusion. 'Haven't you caused enough problems? Just go away.'

'This is important.'

'So is this!'

Toby pulled her arm and was surprised when Hayden grabbed his wrist and yanked him away.

'Hey, bro. Didn't you hear? She wants to be left alone.'

Toby blinked in surprise—then suddenly realized that Hayden had been chatting her up. He looked incredulously between them. Jen had the good sense to blush and look away. Hayden drew himself up to his full height, which was almost a head taller than Toby. Toby couldn't stop himself from laughing at the schoolyard macho display.

'Are you serious?'

'This is downtime, man. Time to chill, respect other

people's personal space and go about your *own* business.'

Toby pushed Hayden aside. 'Jen this is important. It's about NanoMite.'

Hayden was surprised that he'd been shoved aside. 'Dude, that's so uncool!' He grabbed Toby by the scruff of the neck—bad move. Hayden's powers had faded, whereas Toby's were still strong. He effortlessly batted Hayden's arms aside and threw the hero over his shoulder.

Hayden sailed across the control room, crashing down onto a control panel that was covered in paper plates and half empty bottles. He groaned in pain.

Jurgen stepped towards Toby, but stopped when Toby held up his hand threateningly. 'Don't even think about it.'

Jen was apoplectic. 'What are you doing? Have you gone crazy?'

Toby suddenly became aware that everybody was staring at him. He was starting to feel embarrassed.

'This is about us,' he said quietly.

'There is no "us"!'

Toby frowned . . . then the double meaning suddenly dawned on him. His cheeks burned more fiercely as he realized what a jealous idiot he must look like. He had really made a mess of the situation.

'No, no, no! Not like that. I mean our trackers—our

CUCIs. Somebody turned them off. Somebody was trying to get us killed in Brooklyn,' he hissed. She looked uncomprehendingly at him. 'Eric Kirby turned them off! He was trying to kill us!'

A gasp filtered across the room. Toby instantly regretted the outburst.

Jen stared at him with wide disbelieving eyes. 'You are a complete jerk, do you know that? Now, of all times.'

'What do you mean?'

She looked surprised. 'You haven't heard? Where have you been hiding? No, wait, I remember. You're too important to read messages people send you.'

She pushed past Toby and hit an icon on a computer screen. The music faded, and an image of Eric Kirby appeared on the screen. The room was deathly silent.

'This is an official notice to all members of the Hero Foundation. Hard times and difficult decisions have bonded us all together and made us comrades and friends. However, fate has decreed that I should take a different path.'

Toby glanced around the room. Everybody had heard the message before, but they were still glued to the screen.

'Effective immediately, I resign my position as the head of the Foundation. Chameleon was my second in command, but will not be taking the position as leader.

Chaos Effect

It has been a difficult decision, and one I make with a heavy heart. You have all been like a family to me, and I wish you all a very long life.'

The screen blinked out. The room was so quiet that Toby could hear the blood pounding in his ears. Jen stood with her hands on her hips, looking accusingly at Toby.

Toby didn't know what to say. It didn't seem right to accuse Kirby of attempted murder, but what else could he do? He was feeling angry at the injustice of it all. He looked around the control room; they needed to know the truth. His voice trembled from nerves.

'NanoMite is still out there. He's just been spotted in Cairo. It looks like the super-dudes didn't defeat him after all.'

Toby scowled at the crowd, none of whom replied. They just stared at him with open mouths. He slunk out of the control centre without another word. He would have to resolve the situation on his own.

Emily looked around the wreckage of Forge's hideout. It hadn't been much to look at in the first place, but now it was a complete disaster area. Howling wind blew in from sections of the walls and roof that had been torn away. Nothing in the room had escaped destruction.

Pete stood away from her, lost in his own thoughts. Emily stayed tactfully quiet. Finally, Pete spoke up. He sounded weary.

'It's the end of Forge, isn't it?'

Pete glanced at the partially melted huge television set that had been linked to every games console known to man. It had been a great chill-out room for the Forge crew, in between plotting their schemes. Not that there had been great schemes. Under Pete's leadership they had used their powers to simply mess around and have fun—a far cry from Mr Grimm and Momentum's plans for Forge to be a new superpower in the world. They had set up an infrastructure with which they could hack and steal powers from both Hero.com and Villain.net. They had more money than they knew what to do with, and an increasing membership base of disillusioned people from the Foundation and the Council. Things had only taken a serious turn for Forge when Jake Hunter started to blackmail Pete.

Pete's legs were shaking. He was feeling weaker by the hour as the viral bomb Jake had planted inside him destroyed him from the inside. What a waste his time at Forge had been. They could have done something really special with it. Now he was going to die, Forge taken from him, his friends lost, Jake Hunter no longer able to cure him, and a bizarre biomechanical villain pursuing him for his powers. What a mess.

Chaos Effect

'You can still go to the Foundation, Pete. Perhaps they can find a cure?' said Emily optimistically.

'I don't think that's an option any more,' said Pete quietly. 'I wish this hadn't happened. None of it. Finding the stupid website, running in with Basilisk and Viral, getting ill . . . and the whole Jake Hunter thing.' Pete smashed his fist down on the remains of a table—the wood splintered under the impact. 'I wish he had been hit by a car or something!'

'It's all random events, Pete. It's all out of our hands. It's the butterfly effect,' she said with a smile as she recalled something Mr Grimm had said to them a long time ago when they had stopped a boat loaded with pirated DVDs. 'Do you remember?'

Pete's brow knitted together as he tried to recall. Remembering more than several weeks back was difficult. It was as though his overloaded powers blanked his memory. He shook his head.

'In London a butterfly flaps its wings which in turn displaces air particles. Those particles hit others, bouncing like a pinball. One air particle hits two air particles, and they hit another two each, etcetera. It keeps on adding up so by the time those particles have bounced off one another they have travelled halfway around the world and the number of displaced particles has grown to thousands of billions. Enough to cause a cyclone that could devastate China.'

'That's one hell of a lethal butterfly,' murmured Pete. 'They should kill it quick.'

Emily laughed. 'That's exactly what you said to Mr Grimm.'

Pete looked at her with sad eyes. 'I don't remember that. There's a lot I've forgotten.'

'Chaos theory,' said a chillingly familiar voice.

Emily and Pete spun around to see NanoMite peel himself from the wall one atom at a time.

'Wherever you run, I will find you,' he warned. 'It's inevitable, in the same way order arises from chaos.'

'I don't know what you're talking about, freak,' growled Pete as he moved closer to Emily.

'Quantum mechanics is a wonderful toy. Seemingly random events all add up to an inevitable conclusion, only to see that conclusion, you must have superior intellectual power. I have a neural network at my disposal, the very best minds bound together to form the fastest computer network ever.'

'You can't defeat us,' said Emily as threateningly as she could.

'I already have. Chance and chaos have dictated that conclusion.' He fixed his unblinking gaze on Pete. 'Hero.com would not have existed if you hadn't saved Eric Kirby from the jungle during the war. It was your comment that led Kirby to develop Hero.com, which then got copied and pirated by the Council to form

Chaos Effect

Villain.net. You discovered Hero.com just after Jake Hunter found Villain.net thanks to Basilisk. If Hunter hadn't found the website then lightning would never have struck. If Hunter hadn't escaped from Diablo Island, then the fortifications would not have been weak enough for Basilisk to free Viral. If Basilisk hadn't freed Viral, then Lord Eon would not have escaped from his permanent tomb on the island—and you would not have been almost drowned in raw super-powers and therefore would have been unable to travel back in time to save Eric Kirby and give him the idea for Hero.com.'

Pete and Emily swapped a concerned look—Nano-Mite knew everything about them.

'All aided, of course, by random decisions from Kirby and your friends. All chance occurrences that led you to possess the one power I need to destroy humanity and bring to life my army of machines to dominate this world peacefully.'

'I don't know what power you are talking about!' said Pete.

'Your ability to mix the energies inside your body to create specific powers. That will create the perfect replicator for my Swarm! That is the key!'

'You're crazy!' exclaimed Emily. 'How did you come to that conclusion that this is peaceful?'

'When it is just me and my Swarm there will be no

enemy left to face us, therefore the inevitable conclusion is world peace. Life as you know it will be replaced by synthetic life created by me!'

'That sounds like the ramblings of a completely insane maniac!'

Everybody suddenly turned to see Toby standing at the far end of the room. He had jumped down through the shattered portion of roof. He nodded at Pete and Emily. 'Hi, guys.'

'How did you find us?' said Pete in astonishment.

'Probably the same way motor-mouth did, through Emily's CUCI.'

NanoMite glared at Toby. 'You interfere in business that is not yours.'

'What's the matter? Hadn't you planned for me to turn up? Is that just a little too random for you? I know who you really are, Professor Philip Epstein.'

'Epstein is dead!'

'I don't think so. I think he's still inside you, maybe that nagging voice of conscience you still have?'

NanoMite snarled—then suddenly grabbed his head in his hands and bellowed in pain. His entire body shook as if he was being electrocuted.

'Nnnnoooo!' he roared. Then his voice changed, becoming almost human. It was Epstein but he sounded in pain as he duelled with his evil alter ego. 'You must run . . . children . . .'

Chaos Effect

Toby stood his ground. 'We can help you defeat him, Professor!'

'He is too strong . . . argh!' NanoMite dropped to his knees—his voice suddenly switching back, full of mechanical menace. 'Epstein is dead!' He quaked some more as the Epstein personality fought for control. 'If he gets the power from Pete to duplicate the Swarm . . . uh . . . all will be lost! Gah!'

NanoMite fell flat on his back, his legs violently kicking out as if he was suffering a seizure. Partially demolished items around the room were pulverized further. Then he fell still.

After several seconds of silence, Pete spoke up. 'Well, that was weird.'

NanoMite suddenly stood and grabbed Pete around the throat. 'Now you are mine!'

Emily screamed and tried to prise the hand away but it was too strong. NanoMite backhanded her— and Emily flew across the room. She stopped herself dead in the air, centimetres from walloping into the wall.

'Steel fist!' she said. Her Bluetooth headset, discreetly hidden by her blonde hair, pulsed as it received the command and the power was downloaded. Emily shot towards NanoMite at full speed—her arms outstretched.

Just as she was about to impact into the villain

NanoMite's body suddenly parted like curtains and she passed through the hole that had formed in the centre of his body. Emily smashed through the wall, disappearing outside the building.

While Emily had taken the initiative, Pete and Toby hadn't been standing idle.

The pressure NanoMite was exerting on Pete's throat was being absorbed by his body, making him swell twice in size. In seconds he grew half a metre—forcing NanoMite's hand open.

Toby focused his attention on the villain. 'Ice Storm!' he commanded. A blast of ultra-strong hailstones issued from his mouth with such ferocity the walls and ceiling quickly iced over. NanoMite was covered in ice—then his body glowed an intense red as the nanites increased their temperature and the ice instantly turned to steam.

Toby was surprised—it had worked for Jurgen. Then he remembered what Jen had told him, the nanobots share information in a hive mind. Those that had been defeated in Vegas would have passed the information on before they were destroyed. The nanites couldn't be defeated the same way twice—which explained why Emily couldn't ram into him: Jurgen had already done that trick when he hurled the pick-up through the giant nanite construct.

However, the ice distraction forced NanoMite to face

Chaos Effect

Toby—giving Pete the chance to clobber him with a massive fist to the face. It was a basic move, but Pete took satisfaction in knocking NanoMite's head clean off—literally.

The villain's head exploded in a shower of particles that hung in the air. NanoMite stumbled backwards, his hands clawing for a head that wasn't there.

Toby joined Pete—the two friends standing side-by-side once again.

'We still haven't lost that old teamwork, huh?' stated Toby with an edge of relief.

The particle swarm around NanoMite's head suddenly coalesced again and the villain snarled at them.

'How're we going to defeat him?' said Pete in surprise.

NanoMite extended his hands—then was suddenly yanked through the roof by an invisible force. Emily hovered above them, using a telekinetic power to effortlessly lift the fiend.

Toby soared out after her and hovered alongside. For the first time he got a full view of where the Forge nerve-centre was located: it had been built on a giant plateau in the middle of a dramatic mountain range. There was a cool blue sky above and pine trees clinging to the mountain all around. It was breathtakingly beautiful. The moon was massive, hanging in the daytime sky and giving the vista an unreal appearance. That was another cataclysmic event that needed dealing with, and he just hoped that Chameleon had it all in hand. They were high in the Rocky Mountains of Colorado, and it looked just as breathtaking as all the pictures Toby had seen.

Emily grunted as she swept her arms sideways—NanoMite was thrust in the same direction. He smashed into the side of the mountain, causing a trickle of rocks to slide down and part of his body to scatter like grains.

'Tobe, get him!'

The villain tried to stand, but was hampered by the fact his body was still reassembling.

'Laser Vision,' Toby yelled into his headset. Seconds later his vision turned blood red and he squinted just above NanoMite. A stream of red energy blasted from his eyes and exploded in the rock face high above NanoMite.

Pete jumped up through the gap. His increased size meant he couldn't fly like the others, but he was still able to travel in great bounds.

'You missed him!' he screeched.

The rocks Toby had hit suddenly cracked—and dropped straight down onto NanoMite. The landslide lasted for forty seconds, kicking up a plume of dust and echoing between the peaks. It cleared, leaving no sign of the villain.

Chaos Effect

Emily joined Pete and Toby on the Forge rooftop, which was pocked with gaping holes. Pete smiled at Toby's handiwork.

'Not bad.'

'Thanks.' He hesitated, desperate to mend their friendship. 'Pete—'

'Why should we be mates?' said Pete. 'We've been trying to kill each other for ages. Is it because I'm dying? You feel sorry for me now? I don't need sympathy.' The words tumbled out. He actually *did* need sympathy; he just didn't want to ask for it. And in the face of his own mortality, repairing old friendships seemed the right thing to do.

Toby kicked the ground nervously. 'All friends fight, don't they? It's just that not all of them have superpowers. And for your information, I don't feel sorry for you. I just don't see the point in being mad at each other, especially when we're on the same side. More or less.'

Pete stared at him. It was difficult to maintain his fierce expression and his face started splitting into a grin.

'You're not going to get all soppy on me now, are you?'

Toby burst out laughing. Emily joined in; she was relieved to see the two old friends were not beating the stuffing out of one another. Then she quickly sobered up as Pete suddenly grunted and dropped to his knees, clutching his stomach. He threw up blood.

'Tobe, Pete's dying. He's got some bug inside that Jake put in him.'

'Hunter did this to you?'

'We need to get him back to the Foundation and find a cure,' pressed Emily.

Toby nodded. 'We can quantum tunnel him out of here.' He touched his headset to issue the command—just as a massive boulder struck him in the side.

Toby wasn't prepared for the assault. The pain was excruciating as every bone in his right-hand side was shattered. He was forced off the rooftop, falling a dozen metres to the slope below. Fortunately the boulder landed away from him as he rebounded from several trees. The trunk of one particularly tall pine bent back from the impact, but prevented him from rolling further down the steep incline.

He dropped to the foot of the tree and groaned as blood gushed from lacerations on his forehead, stinging his eyes. He could just see the edge of the Forge headquarters sticking out of the plateau, supported on stilts.

NanoMite extracted himself from the landslide in a rapidly condensing cloud of particles. He was still half formed, but managed to unleash an energy blast at Emily. She reeled over the edge of the building at an angle from him, so Toby couldn't see where she landed.

Chaos Effect

Pete suddenly went rigid as the cloud of nanobots engulfed him.

In his daze, Toby felt for his headset. 'Healing . . .' he muttered, but his fingers touched a smashed lump of plastic and components that the boulder had destroyed in a direct impact. He had to rely on the slow inbuilt healing factor within the powers. But that was not going to be enough time to help Pete.

Pete screamed in agony as the nanites entered through his ears, nose, mouth, tear ducts and all the pores in his skin. At first it felt as if he was being sandblasted alive, then the pain turned into a million red-hot needles as the nanobots invaded his body and drilled down— chewing into his bone marrow and infiltrating the very fibres of his DNA, extracting the unique superpowers that had formed in his system.

NanoMite laughed victoriously as his Swarm sucked Pete's powers from his body. Pete deflated as his enlarged bulk slowly reduced back to his normal size like a balloon leaking air. The cyan colour drained from his skin as every vestige of power was removed.

Toby watched his old friend collapse. NanoMite punched the air, whooping like a madman. The Swarm around him suddenly grew in volume as the villain used Pete's stolen abilities to form a bespoke duplication power.

There was no stopping NanoMite now. His army was increasing in size, potentially infinitely large.

Mankind was doomed.

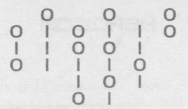

Stooping to His Level

Toby watched in despair as Pete's mass deflated as NanoMite sucked every last molecule of hyper energy from him.

NanoMite roared to the heavens, casting Pete's limp body to one side. NanoMite lolloped towards the satellite dish on top of the Forge headquarters. Even in his groggy state, Toby knew that NanoMite may have got his prize, but he was miles from the main power lines he needed to travel. An internal generator powered the building and the dish was his only immediate way in or out of the Rocky Mountains.

Toby's laser vision had already dissipated from his system. Powers only lasted for a minute when downloaded from the headset, enabling him to download more than the usual three.

His fingers found his phone. Luckily NanoMite was far enough away that it was still working. If he unleashed his Swarm, then the phone would die instantly. The screen was cracked, but viewable, and would allow him to bypass his broken voice-controlled headset. He found the power he needed—it was the last power he would be able to download this cycle.

NanoMite aimed for the huge satellite dish and flexed his body, ready to transform into his particle state and enter the dish. A massive explosion suddenly rocked the rooftop, throwing him off balance. The explosion was so fierce that the entire building suddenly tilted sideways; the satellite dish severed from its base and toppled through the weakened rooftop, thwarting the villain's escape.

Emily hovered over the forest and watched as Toby hurled an intensive fireball at the stilts supporting the Forge headquarters. The wooden struts combusted and the entire building teetered over the plateau—before finally falling onto the steep incline.

It was an amazing sight. The building partially disintegrated from the initial drop. Pine trees pummelled the remainder of the structure as it slid down the incline, gaining momentum and felling some of the mighty trees in its path.

She saw Pete and NanoMite vanish into the wreckage as it crumbled around them. The sliding building was now heading straight for Toby and he didn't look strong enough to get out of the way.

Toby watched as the Forge headquarters formed a

landslide straight for him. He tried to fly, but didn't
have the strength. He slumped against a tree, waiting
for the inevitable.

Emily suddenly swooped down and dragged him
away. Toby was too heavy for her to lift him out of the
landslide's path, and the wreckage was too broad to
sidestep—her only option was to outrun it.

Toby's bum scraped along the steep forest floor as
Emily struggled to drag him. She could only fly a metre
above the ground while holding him and was forced to
slalom between trees. Branches whipped against her
face.

Toby could do nothing but cling on to her arms. The
building was moving faster, inexorably catching them
up.

He craned his head around to talk to her. 'Em! Go
fast—'

A thick tree branch smacked him across the face.

'Sorry!' Emily risked a glance behind them—which
was a bad idea. She flew straight into a tree. The impact
dazed her and she crumpled on top of Toby.

They both watched in horror as the ruin bore down
on them—

Then the twisted wreckage ran out of steam, snag-
ging on trees that would no longer fall. The groaning
building slid to a halt—the partial remains of a door-
frame touched Toby's nose, pressing his face against the

tree. He turned his head sideways convinced that he would be slowly crushed to death . . . but the landslide had stopped.

Toby and Emily extricated themselves from the wreck. Their legs were shaking.

'Need to heal . . . ' gasped Toby, dropping to his knees. Emily pulled out her mobile and called up her last available power to heal Toby. She held the flickering screen close to his face. The power transferred and his wounds slowly bonded together. Eventually he stood up, although his legs still felt wobbly.

'Did I get him?'

'Yes. But you also got Pete,' Emily replied in a flat voice.

He shot her a look loaded with concern—then scurried up the incline, searching through the debris.

'Pete? Pete?' he screamed, dropping to all-fours to clamber up the steep mountainside.

Emily took to the air and surveyed the trail of destruction. She spotted something. 'Over here!' She swooped down to a leg poking from the remains of one room.

Toby quickly joined her and they pulled the plasterboard off Pete. He was motionless, his skin pale from plaster dust.

Toby felt his stomach knot in concern. 'Is he alive?'

Emily checked for a pulse. 'I don't know.' She pressed

her cheek close to his mouth to feel for any signs of breath. 'I don't think he's breathing!'

'Download a healing power!'

'I used the last one on you!' Toby didn't blame her for her angry tone.

Pete suddenly groaned and moved his head slightly. Emily yelped with delight and Toby closed his eyes in silent thanks.

'What happened?' Pete asked in a weak voice.

'You brought the house down, pal,' laughed Toby.

Pete pushed himself upright and squinted at them.

'You shouldn't move,' Emily cautioned. 'You could have a back injury. Can you move your legs?' Pete kicked both legs. She remembered hearing that from a hospital TV show; it was supposed to be a good sign.

'I can't see properly . . . and I think I broke a rib. It hurts when I breathe.'

'You haven't got your glasses,' Toby pointed out. Then he remembered that Pete had used his own high-intensity healing power to cure his shortsightedness. He exchanged a worried look with Emily.

Emily gently squeezed his hand. 'We think Nano-Mite drained you of all your powers. Maybe you're back to normal.'

They couldn't read the expression on Pete's face—was it disappointment or relief?

'Just when I needed them to heal me,' he gasped.

Then the sound of pouring sand got their attention. Dust was shifting from the debris field, gathering at one central point. They knew it was the nanites, spread across the landslide, reforming NanoMite.

'Is there no way to kill him?' said Emily in despair.

'It doesn't look like it,' muttered Toby. Then with a sinking feeling he added, 'How's your teleport power?'

'Still recharging. Yours?'

Toby didn't have to reply, the look on his face told Emily it was the same story. 'That means we're trapped out here with him until we recharge.' He grabbed Pete's arm and pulled him up.

Pete screamed out, clutching his ribs. 'OW!'

'Sshh!' hissed Toby urgently. 'We've got to get out of here now!'

Emily took Pete's weight on the other side and they headed into the trees, hoping NanoMite couldn't find them in the wilderness.

They had been travelling down the mountain for almost thirty minutes when they stopped at a fast-flowing stream to drink water. It was cool, refreshing, and it even stopped Pete's constant griping.

Emily commented that she felt that her teleportation power was almost recharged, but remained cautious, as she would need it at full strength to get the three of them out in one jump. Toby still had another several minutes before his charge would be sufficiently strong to jump them out. They could then return to hunt down the stranded NanoMite in force, before he reached any technology to escape.

Toby had used the time to enquire about Lorna. Emily had assured him that she was safe and well, even if she was with Hunter. That worried Toby, but Emily squeezed his hand and told him not to worry. Lorna knew what she was doing.

Toby pulled out his phone and held it high for a signal. It was a satellite phone and didn't rely on traditional cellular towers.

'What are you doing?' asked Emily as she stretched on the cool grass and enjoyed the warm sun.

'Seeing if I can call Jen for help. She's not picking up.' Then he remembered this was Kirby's phone and didn't blame her for avoiding a call from him after he had just quit the Foundation in its time of need. Toby was feeling bitter towards the old man. He had trusted him with his own safety, and in return Kirby had tried to kill him to prevent him from revealing his past misdeeds.

He noticed the flashing unread mail icon was still at the bottom of the screen. Now it looked as if Kirby wasn't going to get his phone back, he didn't mind snooping in his personal files.

He was surprised to see the message was from Eric Kirby. The subject was FAO: TOBY WILKINSON.

FAO—'for the attention of'. Why would Kirby send him a message? Perhaps it was an apology—not that saying sorry would ever absolve him. Toby opened the message and a video file started playing. Kirby himself recorded it as he was walking.

'Toby, if you are watching this then you are alive and my faith in you wasn't misplaced.' That comment bemused him, it was the last thing he had expected to hear. Kirby paused and looked around with a worried expression before continuing. 'I hope, by now, you have traced NanoMite's identity. You may be wondering why I sent you on this path rather than tell you from the beginning.'

'You got that right,' mumbled Toby. Emily and Pete were now peering over his shoulder to watch the message.

'I did it because you had to discover the facts for yourself. I could not bring myself to execute my friend, nor could I order you to. But now, you know what needs to be done. I have done many things I am proud of, and many I am not. The Foundation had been pressured to get results from Philip, Professor Epstein, I mean. Pete Kendall and Jake Hunter were proving too much of a threat . . . '

'Cool,' said Pete. Emily shushed him.

' . . . to the Foundation, the Council, and to mankind. They had to be neutralized. The nanobot technology was the last step I could take before the Inner Circle demanded their execution. I was doing it to save their lives because they were my mistakes. Pete, because of what I put him through, and Hunter, indirectly, because I didn't stop him when I should have. You were right in saying we should have brought down the Council of Evil. The reason I said no was because of an old pact between the two sides. By honouring that pact I allowed Jake to run wild and cause the mayhem he did. He could have been like you . . . '

'Who are the Inner Circle?' asked Pete.

Kirby looked up sharply, a worried expression on his face as he searched for something they couldn't see. His voice dropped in volume. 'I haven't got time to tell you about the Inner Circle,' he said as if he'd heard, 'because, by the time you watch this, I will be dead. Sacrifices have to be made for the greater good and I sacrifice myself to stop the Dark Hunter.' The news hit Toby like a physical blow. He heard Emily gasp. 'Your primary concern is NanoMite. If he ever gets hold of Pete Kendall, then he will be able to mine the powers from his body and absorb them. You must stop this happening at all costs otherwise NanoMite will be almost indestructible!'

Toby closed his eyes. Why hadn't he watched the

message earlier when he had first seen it? He knew why: he had been too angry with Kirby to bother.

Kirby continued. 'I had to disable the CUCI within you and Jen as the nanites were locking onto the signal and using it to follow you. It was the only way I could help you avoid his clutches without attracting the attention of the Inner Circle. Without the information in the journal I doubt you would have pieced everything together and the Inner Circle forbade me to help you directly. It would have upset the pact; upset the balance between good and evil. I had to maintain the appearance of honouring the agreement. I had to maintain this illusion because I am about to face Jake Hunter, which directly violates everything I had agreed with the Council.' Toby wanted to kick himself. He had been furious with Kirby for all the wrong reasons . . . well, mostly wrong. 'You must find Pete and place him in protection, or worse case, destroy him.'

Pete snorted indignantly—which sent a stabbing pain to his ribs. 'That's nice of him!'

'You *have* been a bit of a handful,' Emily countered.

Kirby stopped walking so the image became more stable. He looked around again, his voice dropping to a whisper. 'The only way to fight NanoMite is—'

He looked up and the video suddenly ended.

'Is that it?' Emily asked in alarm.

Stooping to His Level

Toby thumbed through the message again. 'That's it. That's all he said.'

'What does that mean?'

Toby rubbed his forehead, he was starting to get a headache. 'It means we've failed. NanoMite's got what he wants.'

'But we can still stop him getting away,' said Emily, ever the optimist.

Toby nodded. 'I suppose so.'

Branches suddenly cracked, sending them all on edge. They stared at the trees. *Something* was moving.

'I think we should leave,' whispered Toby.

'I can't . . . not yet,' warned Emily. She just intuitively knew she needed a little longer to restore her teleport ability.

The trees shook—then NanoMite strode out from the forest.

'You mortals tire. I do not! Thanks to my stolen powers, I can now do anything!' He held up his hand and looked at it. Ice started to cover it, then that vaporized as lightning bolts crackled from his fingertips, then his forearm morphed into a long set of spiralling blades that spun at high speeds. 'I am not hindered by your weak bodies, there is no limit to the power I can wield!'

'Em?' wailed Toby.

'Not yet!'

The branches behind NanoMite shook and a massive

cloud rose behind him—it was a colossal swarm of nanites. The trees were suddenly shredded as if an army of termites had gnawed their way through in seconds. A mile-long stretch of destroyed forest now lay behind NanoMite.

'My Swarm duplicates with each passing hour. Soon I will have enough nanites to raze the world and rebuild everything in my image!'

'That would be one ugly world,' quipped Toby. Only by keeping the fiend talking could they hope Emily's power would be restored in time.

NanoMite glowered at Toby. 'Your death will be the most painful.' NanoMite suddenly clutched his head. 'Nnnooo!!'

He started beating his own head as Epstein's voice forced its way out. 'The only way to defeat me . . . is by dropping to my level . . . argh!'

NanoMite roared in anger. 'Epstein is dead!' he roared.

The noise was attracting movement to Toby's side. NanoMite was too busy clawing at his own head to remove the voice. He didn't see a huge grizzly bear storm out of the forest, fleeing from the Swarm. It almost barrelled straight into Toby—then stopped and reared on its hind legs, towering over him as it roared.

Toby staggered back in surprise, dropping his phone.

Stooping to His Level

Then he acted on impulse. He had no desire to hurt the bear, but they needed a distraction if they were going to survive the encounter with NanoMite.

His super-strength surged through his muscles—the power was seconds away from disappearing. He just had enough time to grab the surprised bear by the leg and fling the animal into NanoMite.

Half of NanoMite's body exploded into granules as the enraged bear took him by surprise and lashed out at the supervillain.

'Emily, get us outta here!' screamed Toby.

Emily grabbed him by the scruff of the neck and clung on to Pete with her other hand. 'Let's go!'

BOOM! The three teenagers suddenly vanished in a thunderclap.

By the time NanoMite had reformed, his Swarm had made short work of the bear. The villain didn't care about the humans; he had what he needed and they couldn't stop him now. All he had to do was find his way back to civilization. Something caught his attention on the ground. He stalked forwards and picked up Toby's mobile phone. The nanites automatically restored power to the device as he held it up.

It still had a signal.

NanoMite's laugh echoed off the mountain peaks. He had just been handed an escape route from the wilderness.

* * *

Emily's first thought of a destination was home—so the three of them teleported into her driveway. Toby looked around in panic, remembering the last time he had been in their town. Now it looked worse.

A fine grey dust covered everything and blotted out the sun. They looked underfoot and realized the dust was a fine metallic powder. A second look around revealed that dozens of buildings had been chewed away. Power pylons had been dissolved, some still partially poking from the dust. The scene looked apocalyptic.

Toby knew from what he'd read about Project Swift that all it would take was a charge of nanites to bond the dust together to create a layer of synthetically 'alive' metal that would choke plant and animal life, rendering the world uninhabitable.

Pete collapsed, weakened by the teleport. They needed to get him to a hospital.

The sight of five synthesized humans, enslaved by technology grafted to their faces, was enough to propel Toby into action.

'Is that Mr Patel?' asked Emily as the figures ran towards them.

Toby didn't bother answering, although he was relieved to see that Jurgen hadn't killed his old boss.

Stooping to His Level

He grabbed Emily and Pete as he felt his own teleport power finally recharge and he headed to the one safe destination he could think of.

As soon as they arrived at the Foundation Hospital, the very one where Pete had awoken from his coma and escaped, Toby sensed the sombre mood. News of Kirby's death had already reached everybody. Nobody could get in touch with Chameleon, which left the organization rudderless.

Pete was immediately taken into care and Toby's and Emily's minor wounds were dealt with.

Emily stayed at Pete's side, but Toby preferred to pace the corridor outside the ward. His thoughts had strayed to Lorna. During their trek through the forest, Emily had told him how Lorna had set out to persuade Jake from his path of destruction, helped by using the powers on Toby's phone. Emily hadn't heard from her for a couple of days and was worried sick. That didn't help Toby's mood.

He was surprised when Jen arrived; the Foundation headquarters were in a different location from the command centre so somebody must have informed her of his return. She still looked annoyed and demanded to know why Toby hadn't been answering his phone. Toby coolly pointed out that he had lost his phone and had been using Kirby's. He didn't see the point in keeping it secret from her now that Kirby was dead, Chameleon was AWOL, and his sister was still with Jake Hunter. This shut Jen up and she had the good grace to look humbled.

'Sorry,' she mumbled.

'What was that?'

Her eyes narrowed as she looked at him. Her voice became clearer. 'You heard me. I'm sorry you made me think you were a jerk!'

Toby blinked, trying to work out if that was an apology or another insult. She smiled and suddenly gave him a hug. Toby was too surprised to say anything.

Jen composed herself. 'You were right about Nano-Mite, he's still loose.'

'We know where he is: the Rockies. We can stop him.'

'That's not an option any more. He got into the communications system and escaped from the wilderness.'

'How?' The moment the word was out of his mouth, Toby's hand snapped down to the pocket where his phone should be. It was conspicuously empty. He sagged, feeling defeated.

Jen hadn't noticed. She pressed on. 'He's started to take the military out. Hayden, Jurg, and a bunch of others have been trying to take him out, but it's proving impossible. With nobody here to figure things out . . . we're at a loss.'

Toby sighed. Every moment was precious, but he couldn't think how they could defeat a seemingly unstoppable terror.

A doctor poked his head from Pete's room. 'He's awake if you want to speak to him.'

Pete was sitting upright in bed, greedily eating from a bowl of strawberries and cream. He looked the picture of health, sporting thick replacement glasses on his nose. He grinned at Toby when he entered. Jen kept close to the door, she only knew the darker side of Pete.

'You look . . . normal,' said Toby in surprise. And he meant it. The disgusting cracked cyan skin had vanished, a side effect from the quantity of powers he had ingested.

'I feel great,' he exclaimed. 'Doctors said every trace of my powers have been removed. Everything! Those nanites cleansed my system completely clean. They're brilliant.'

'That's what they were designed for. What about the virus thing Jake put inside you?'

'Gone!'

Emily whooped with delight and hugged Pete. 'So you're not going to die?'

'Not yet,' beamed Pete. 'It's all gone. The doctors said it was attached to my powers. I'm back to normal!'

* * *

In the dark depths of the Atlantic Ocean, a US Navy Ohio Class submarine prowled through the waters. The USS Michigan was a ballistic submarine and had been on routine patrol until they had received orders to prime their weapons and decrease their depth as a standby to firing its nuclear payload.

On board, the crew were tense and nervous. This didn't feel like one of the many drills they performed to stay in peak fighting condition. This felt real.

Captain Freeman had been in constant touch with command, but was no wiser about why they were on active standby. One order that had seemed particularly bizarre was they had to shoot at the *moon*. He didn't share that with the rest of the crew in case they thought he had gone crazy.

However, for the last thirty minutes, command had fallen silent and he was starting to fear the worst. Surely a world war couldn't have broken out so rapidly? After fifteen more minutes of radio silence he ordered the craft to surface so they could establish satellite communication.

The sleek submarine broke through the unusually millpond-still ocean surface with all the menace of a shark's fin. Captain Freeman was faced with the further dilemma of being unable to uplink with any satellites.

Stooping to His Level

He was pondering what his next step should be when a piercing electric shriek rang through the boat. All the electrical systems suddenly overloaded, control panels sparked, and the craft plunged into darkness.

After several moments the lighting suddenly flicked back on and the crew burst into chatter. No system was responding to their commands. The helm was unresponsive, leaving them drifting in the ocean.

The captain looked around in alarm as the boat suddenly changed course and every weapon armed itself. In one brief cyber attack, nanites had seized control of the nuclear submarine—in fact, every military asset around the world.

Mankind had lost the ability to fight back.

Pete and Emily continued chatting happily away. Toby peered out of the window. He was so lost in thought that he jumped when Jen spoke close to his shoulder.

'What's on your mind? I thought you'd be happy you got your friend back?'

Toby was happy Pete was alive and well, but he wondered just how safe their friendship was after everything that had happened.

Jen's phone bleeped and she read the message. 'NanoMite has taken control of the world's military.'

'The entire world's?' Toby repeated in shock. Jen nodded. Toby rested his head against the glass with a thud. He wished his old team were together again— Lorna, Emily, and Pete. They always had solutions for impossible problems.

Emily suddenly called from Pete's bedside. 'Toby? I've just got a message from Lorna.'

'Is she OK?'

Emily nodded and Toby was flooded with relief. 'But she needs my help.'

'I'm coming with you.'

'You can't. What about NanoMite?'

'What about him? There's nothing I can do and the awesome twins are dealing with that,' he added ironically, casting a look at Jen. She didn't enjoy the joke.

'There is something you can do. I've been thinking about what NanoMite said . . . or rather the other guy, personality, whoever he was. He said: "drop to his level".'

'I don't know what that means? Does it mean stoop to become a psycho supervillain?'

'I think he meant fight NanoMite on his own terms, at his own level.' Toby still looked blank. Emily smiled. 'Tobe, you have to shrink down to get inside him. Defeat the nanobots face-to-face, and you defeat him.'

Stooping to His Level

Toby looked at her incredulously. 'That must be the most nutty idea you have ever had.'

'I'll come with you,' stated Pete, leaping out of bed.

Toby raised his hand. 'You're not going anywhere. You're officially retired.' Pete scowled, but didn't argue. 'How can we beat somebody who has every power Pete had, can control any piece of technology and tear apart anything, and learns from mistakes so we can't try the same attack twice? Even if we could shrink to his level, and I haven't seen any powers online to let us do that, what could we do to him?'

'We should just drop a nuclear bomb on him,' said Pete. 'The EMP blast from that would wipe him and the nanobots out.'

'We can't. NanoMite controls the world's military. We're the last line of defence.'

Nobody said a word. They were all lost in thought. Finally, Emily spoke up, a gleam in her eye.

'You know, we should fight fire with fire.' She quickly outlined her plan. Toby, Pete, and Jen made inspirational suggestions and tweaks so finally the two-stage plan to assault NanoMite in his lair actually looked achievable. The first part depended on putting his Swarm out of action, and as far as Jen could see, that was the riskiest element.

'That's a long shot,' said Jen finally.

'It's still a chance,' said Toby. 'And it beats not doing anything.'

Jen forced a smile. 'I guess you're right. Count me in.'

Toby nodded solemnly—all they had to do now was find a way to shrink themselves.

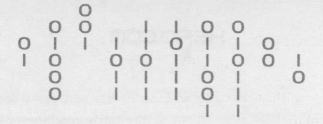

Ever Decreasing Circles

Across the world, cities faced the wrath of NanoMite's Swarm.

London: the power outages spread across the city and out into the suburbs, followed moments later by a fine wave of silver mist that rolled across the landscape. When it had cleared, the terrain was covered in a fine metallic dust that clung to every available surface.

Minutes later an electrical bolt charged through the dust shroud, activating the billions of dormant nanobots held within it. People traipsing home were suddenly attacked as metal tendrils lashed out, over-powering them.

New York: residents reacted with panic to the for-midable dust cloud that rolled through the concrete canyons, clinging to every available surface. They had just recovered from that last outage and watched the new developments with growing trepidation ...

Madrid: the cloud of micro-machines swept in from

the north of the city, smothering business parks and turning busy roads silent as the micro-machines absorbed any form of electrical current in the vicinity.

Motorists on the A-1 *autovia* climbed from their crippled vehicles. Some tried to wipe the dust off their windscreens, but it was a futile gesture. The moment the bots were activated the vehicles were absorbed, steadily melting into the road until nothing remained. People screamed and tried to flee as snaking tentacles reached out to snatch them.

'The East Coast of America and half of Western Europe has already fallen,' commented Jen as she analysed the data in the command centre.

They had returned to Hero HQ together, leaving Pete, who was desperate to get back into action, in the hospital with Emily by his side. The nurses had insisted she'd done enough. In the command centre it almost looked like business as usual if the empty bottles, plastic cups, pizza boxes, and party streamers were ignored.

Technicians gave Toby a cold look and tried to blank him. His wrongful accusations about Kirby came too close to the news of their leader's death, and it would take more than an apology for Toby to undo the ill will.

With nobody to stop him, Toby had had the rare chance to look through the Power Archive, a list of every raw power and its effect. Normally this information was reserved for the commanding officers of the Foundation, but as far as he could see, he and Jen were the most qualified people to hand.

He was surprised to see the same powers had slightly different effects depending on their dosage. Hero.com delivered the same dose across the board. Toby could see many more advantages if they could be administered on a sliding scale. He was also shocked to discover just how many powers had been banned or removed from 'active service' for various reasons.

He scanned through the list and felt a wave of relief—the shrink power was one such prohibited ability. Rather than download it directly into his body, Toby had taken a new phone from the Foundation's supply room and ensured it was loaded up with a series of essential powers.

Jen was busy recruiting volunteers for their plan, and once Toby had selected the exact powers they required, he would clone them onto everybody else's phone.

A quick visit to the research and development department gave him the chance to look through the range of superpowered gadgets available. He selected a particularly cool looking rifle that allowed small glass cartridges of superpowers to be loaded, and the power fired. That left Toby and his assault team free to download other powers into their bodies.

Meanwhile, Jen had been trying to locate NanoMite's stronghold. His Swarm would soon learn the nature of their attack, so they had to be swift and decisive when striking the villain.

That proved to be surprisingly straightforward. Before the satellites had all died, technicians had spotted NanoMite's telltale nanotech energy signature emanating from a single location in the south-east of France, on the banks of the river Rhône. Closer inspection revealed a structure that looked perfect, but when Toby saw what it was, he was not terribly happy about going in.

'We have to,' insisted Jen. 'How else are we going to get close to him?'

'Jen, it's a nuclear reactor!'

'It's a *decommissioned* reactor. The French Government closed the *Superphénix* down in 1996!'

'I don't care! It's still going to be radioactive!'

'Not everywhere.'

Toby searched for another excuse. 'Those people he kidnapped. He said he was using them as a neural network. It they're there when we go storming in, we could injure them! And Emily and Pete told us about the Cohort kids he's using as guards. I don't want to have to blow them away to get to NanoMite.'

Jen hesitated. He had a point.

'We have to be smart about this,' said Toby as he

paced the room. 'We get inside the Swarm with the least possible risk to ourselves, so we can't go jumping right in the middle of NanoMite's operation. We have to take the Swarm out first.'

'How?'

Toby stopped pacing, a calculating grin spreading across his face.

'I have an idea. We'll head them off at the pass!'

NanoMite watched his zombified neural-network hive-mind process the intricate billions of commands needed to control his ever-expanding Swarm. He had replicated the nanites in their hundreds of trillions, so the calculations were supremely complex and beyond any ordinary computer's abilities, and even exceeded his own skills. He'd been forced to kidnap extra mathematicians to increase the hive-mind. Now, all he had to do was sit back and terraform the world into an industrial wasteland.

Occasionally the nagging voice of Professor Epstein would try and seize his conscience, but it was getting easier to fight him off. With each passing hour the Epstein personality was getting weaker—when it had vanished for good he would have no other opposition.

The data his Swarm relayed was processed by the hive-mind into tiny pieces of information he could easily digest. He could access visual and auditory information from any element of his Swarm—and what he saw was total, inevitable victory. He was bringing the world out of chaos and into unified mechanical order.

'Did you have to tell those two?' said Toby in a low disapproving voice.

'Give them a break,' groaned Jen. 'We needed volunteers, and after your outburst, few people wanted to come with you.'

They watched Jurgen and Hayden crouch low in the ditch. Next to them were two girls and three boys, who all had guns strapped across their backs, and identical phones laden with additional powers. They were all Downloaders who had volunteered for the hazardous mission because they still had respect for Toby, and loved the chance to work with the two charismatic twins. Toby couldn't match their names to their faces from the hasty introductions, other than one of them was called Tony, which Jurgen had found highly amusing and kept telling people about the 'two Tonys', pointing between Tony and Toby.

Toby reasoned that entering the nanite Swarm from its leading edge, as it expanded across the continents, would be a safer proposition than appearing in the centre of the mass—but enter it they must if they wanted to neutralize the nanites. They tracked the edge of the Swarm as it moved across Europe.

Jurgen panicked when he saw the nanites were encroaching upon his town in Northern Germany. He pleaded with Toby that they should head there to cut the Swarm off. Toby couldn't argue: any part of the leading edge was an appropriate infiltration point.

Toby had only found enough shrinking power for a single dose each, and that had depleted the Foundation's reserves. There could be no mistakes otherwise NanoMite would be unstoppable.

They had all quantum tunnelled from the Foundation moments before the Swarm had descended, swiftly overrunning the base. There was no going back, no last minute checks. The improvised plan Toby, Emily, Pete, and Jen had formed had to work.

Now they found themselves lying in a damp ditch in Germany, opposite Jurgen's house. Luckily the residents had fled ahead of the techno-storm, so the small traditional village was deathly quiet.

Time seemed to drag as they waited for the Swarm to approach. A fine fog had started to descend, which Toby had initially mistaken for the start of the attack. The fog hampered visibility, making it impossible to see the approaching threat.

'Coming here was a bad idea,' muttered Toby. 'We should move further back, out of this fog.'

'What's that noise?' exclaimed one of the girls suddenly. She peeked above the ditch and looked around. 'It's coming from Jurg's house!'

They strained to listen, and Toby wondered if she'd downloaded super-hearing, which meant she had heard his grumbling all this time. Then they all heard faint barking.

Jurgen's eyes went wide. 'Sable!' He leapt to his feet—Jen and Toby reached out to drag him back down.

'What're you doing?' hissed Toby.

'Sable is my dog! They left her behind!' he said, referring to his mother and stepfather. He broke free from their grasp and ran for the house.

Hayden followed him. 'Dude! Wait!'

A thunderous expression crossed Toby's face; already the plan was beginning to unravel. Before he could complain, Jen held up her finger to silence him.

'Don't say a word,' she threatened. 'I'll bring them back.'

'I'll go,' growled Toby. 'Stay with the others.'

For once, Jen didn't argue. Toby sprinted towards the house as Jurgen opened the door and disappeared inside, shouting his dog's name.

The house was spacious and modern inside, completely opposite to the quaint traditional exterior. A staircase led to the basement, another upstairs. He could see no sign of the twins.

Ever Decreasing Circles

'Jurg? Where are you?'

A fresh bout of barking and excited muffled talking came from upstairs. Toby ascended to find the twins standing in Jurgen's bedroom, stroking an overexcited black Labrador.

'He was trapped in here!' exclaimed Jurgen. 'Look how happy he is!'

'I'm so happy for you,' said Toby sarcastically. Sable scampered to Toby, placing his paws on his chest and delivering a gooey slurp across Toby's face. He tried to fend the hyperactive dog away.

'He likes you, Tony!'

'Get him off me!' Toby was feeling irritated. 'Now can we go back outside and get ready for the mission?'

Hayden pulled Sable off Toby. 'What about the dog? He can't come on the mission, unless, you know, he's some kind of super mutt?'

'*Ja! Ja!* Super-dog, I like this!' chirped Jurgen.

Toby couldn't believe how immature the guys were acting. They still didn't seem to appreciate the danger they were in. 'No! Absolutely not!'

'Then what're we gonna do with him?' asked Hayden.

Before Toby could think of a response, Sable leapt up to lick Hayden's face. The dog's scrambling paw raked across Hayden's touchscreen phone tucked in his shirt pocket and accidentally activated the powers he had lined up to use.

The screen flickered—a whirlwind-like cone of energy swelled out, sweeping the room and searching for living hosts. Sable yelped and raced out of the room—the three heroes were not so lucky.

Toby saw the searching tip of the whirlwind face him and he felt himself sucked into it. His stomach lurched and he experienced a peculiar falling sensation that felt as if it would never end . . .

Then he hit the ground with a thump. His head pounded from the worst headache he'd ever had. It was difficult to stand, but he managed it, wobbling on his feet. Jurgen and Hayden were still there.

'Er, guys . . . where are we?' asked Hayden as he looked around.

For several moments Toby mistook the floor for knee-high grass and the surrounding monoliths that stretched to the white sky far above, for smooth canyon walls, but now he realized what they were—furniture.

'Hayden, you moron! You've shrunk us!'

Hayden grabbed his phone—the dog had cracked the screen. 'This is bogus! It's bust-up.'

'That's your full charge of the power—we don't have any more left to spare for you!'

Panic crossed Hayden's face. 'So I'll be like this, like, for ever?'

'No, it will wear off and you should spring back to normal. The problems are—we're still not small enough to face the nanites, your dosage was split between the three of us; and we're not in position outside!' The plan was falling apart before it had even begun.

Toby pulled his own phone out and thumbed Jen's number. Nothing happened. He stared at the screen. 'I can't get a signal. I think we're too small to pick up the phone's wavelengths.' He gritted his teeth, determined not to shout at the twins for ruining yet another mission.

'I don't think that is our biggest problem,' said Jurgen suddenly.

'"Biggest". Is that supposed to be a joke?'

Then he noticed that Jurgen was staring over his shoulder. Toby slowly turned, dreading what he was going to see.

A monstrous spider was advancing towards them. It would have been small if he had been normal size. At about the size of a coin, it was as large as a van to them now.

They ran through the carpet, but the fibres were as thick as their arms and made progress difficult. The spider didn't seem to have such problems as its eight eyes detected movement, hairs on its legs picked up the subtle vibrations.

Toby suddenly came to his senses and used one of the downloaded powers his body had absorbed. He took flight as the gnashing arachnid fangs sliced towards him.

For some reason the twins hadn't downloaded that power, and became the spider's prey of choice. Toby hovered over the beast and fired a stream of lightning from his fingertips. That got the spider's attention.

Had he been normal size, the charge would have looked like nothing more than a few tiny sparks, but scaled down the effect was much more impressive. The thick lightning crackled around the spider's body—leaping from its legs as the charge was earthed. It was enough to make it stop pursuing the twins—instead it reared up towards Toby.

The monster balanced on its rear legs and stretched out. Toby hadn't been expecting it to reach so high, but the legs were three times longer than its body, so the creature's reach was deceptive. The legs were tipped with nasty looking claws about the size of two fingers together. The claw ripped through Toby's jacket and into his side. He howled in pain as he was plucked from the air and driven into the floor.

He had increased his healing factor, so the wound was already mending—unfortunately it was healing around the spider's leg, which was caught in the flesh around his waist. The spider shook its leg to jolt him free, but Toby was caught fast and found himself being repeatedly bashed against the floor.

Jurgen's and Hayden's reactions were synchronized. They both hurled fire at the arachnid. The flames sloshed from the palms of their hands like liquid napalm. The spider instantly ignited and scuttled in circles as it thrashed in pain—that didn't help Toby's situation. He was trampled under the burning creature's panicked footfalls. Only by gripping the leg and sliding it from his gut could he free himself. The wound quickly healed and Toby was forced to run under the flaming legs to escape.

By the time he looked round, the spider was lying on its back, dead. The flames extinguished themselves with nothing left to burn.

'Are you OK, Tony?'

Toby nodded and reluctantly thanked the twins. 'That was . . . quick thinking. Thanks.'

'There will be more spiders,' warned Jurgen with a sense of urgency. 'This is the countryside. We get many.'

'Terrific!' he exclaimed. 'We don't have time for that. We need to get to Jen. Can't you guys fly?'

Hayden shrugged. 'Thought we wouldn't need it.'

Toby was speechless. During training he had drummed into them that it was the one most useful power available.

'Maybe we can download it?' suggested Jurgen going for his phone. Then he hesitated. 'Oh, I forget. No signal this small.'

'That's right, genius,' said Toby. 'You guys wait here

and try not to get eaten. I'm going to fly up to the window and try and get Jen's attention.'

Toby soared up the vast smooth edifice of Jurgen's wooden desk—it seemed as tall as a skyscraper. He flew over the contents—a laptop, pens and scraps of paper, euro coins and a half empty glass of cola that had almost congealed into syrupy ooze.

He landed on the painted window ledge and peered out of the huge glass pane. He could see the tops of his team's heads, although the mist prevented any clear definition.

'Jen!' His voice sounded pathetically small even to him.

He kicked himself for not downloading an extra growth power to allow them to revert to normal size rather than have to wait for the shrink effect to wear off naturally. That left one option, he would have to fly across to Jen and hope she didn't swat him to death.

Flying back through the house would be time consuming. He was sure the front door had closed behind him and had no idea how he could open it. The most direct exit lay through the window, but it was too big to break. Toby was frustrated, opening a door and breaking a window—two basic tasks that were almost impossible for him to do!

He placed his hands flat on the glass and concentrated

Ever Decreasing Circles

on focusing his lightning blast on melting a hole through the window.

He didn't see the shape slowly moving across the desk behind him.

'They've been gone too long,' said Jen with concern.

'I can't hear any noise inside . . . just the dog,' reported the girl with the acute hearing. 'Something must have happened to them.'

Jen silently agreed, and it had to happen to the twins. After they had gone to rescue the dog, she was slowly coming around to Toby's line of thinking about them. It was a combination of being accident-prone and luck that had portrayed them as great heroes. She was certain that something had gone wrong, and it had been their fault.

'What do we do?' asked the boy who could have been Tony.

'The plan stays the same,' said Jen confidently, although she wasn't feeling so certain inside. 'We enter the Swarm, shrink down, neutralize it then get to NanoMite before he can reactivate them.'

Then something near the houses caught her attention. Something was moving.

* * *

The glass under Toby's hands became warm and soft. A charred black circle started to appear. In a few seconds he would have created a hole big enough to climb through.

Something suddenly thudded against the glass, forcing him to jump backwards. At first he thought a fly had landed on the outside of the window—but it was a metal sphere, the size of his head. Multiple arachnid-like legs covered the surface, attaching it to the glass. It was a nanite. This close he could see the smooth metal surface was criss-crossed with circuit-board-like channels through which energy occasionally pulsed.

It was joined by others of varying sizes, most of which were smaller than the first. In seconds, the entire window was covered, blotting out the light. There were dozens of designs, each capable of doing slightly different tasks. Toby had to peer closely to see the smaller ones, no bigger than the tiniest pores on his shrunken nose.

Some had tiny hair-like sensors covering their bodies, communicating with the other bots. Some had tiny mechanical claws to grip things. Others had an assortment of drilling implements the like of which belonged in a deranged dentist's surgery.

They occasionally moved, twitching left or right. The motion rippled through the Swarm as each machine mirrored the other.

Ever Decreasing Circles

Toby took a step back. He gripped the gun strap that crossed his chest, finding some comfort in knowing he still had his primary weapon, but he was still too big to carry out the plan, and now he was separated from his team by a road that was the scale equivalent of a mile across.

He dropped down off the window ledge and onto the desk, moving slowly so as not to attract the attention of the machine. He backed into a pen that came up to his thigh. He turned—and saw another spider was standing stationary at the end of the desk. This one was huge—twice the size of the one they had killed. Possibly it was an angry parent.

Toby's blood ran cold. All his powers and weapons had been tailored for a mechanical foe. It had taken the twins' combined efforts to defeat the other beast. He hoped that the nanites had got its attention.

He took a side step—and the spider tracked his movement. So much for the idea it was watching the machines rain down outside. He looked around for something he could use as a weapon.

He darted to the side. The spider hadn't been expecting the sudden movement and sprang for the pen, its fangs bouncing off the plastic case and splashing poison.

Toby headed for a stack of books that had been piled higgledy-piggledy; the overlapping covers provided narrow crevasses that the spider couldn't reach. Toby pressed his body in as far as he could.

'Jurg! Hayden!' he screamed, but his companions didn't respond.

The spider threw itself with fury at the books. Its bloated body couldn't make it through the gap between the narrow volumes. Fangs, dripping with paralysing poison, slashed close to Toby's face and he could smell the sharp acrid odour of the creature.

He was trapped, and the Swarm was no doubt attacking his friends outside—he could ill afford this struggle. He was angry with himself, why had he followed the twins inside? Why had he allowed them to come at all?

His anger built until he could hold back his temper no more. He booted the spider in the cephalothorax, which was the nearest thing it had to a head, with all the enhanced strength he could muster. The arthropod toppled onto its back, eight legs cycling the air as it fought to right itself.

Toby rolled from concealment and flew across the desk to the cola filled glass. He grunted as he gripped the glass lip and strained to topple it. It was like moving a house . . . but his super-strength gradually tilted the glass until gravity took over and it toppled onto the desk. The sticky cola residue splashed out just as the spider flipped upright and scuttled towards him. The gunk stuck to its leg hairs, slowing it down, as though it was walking through treacle.

'Gotcha!' yelled Toby.

But the spider wasn't finished with him. It angled its abdomen and a strand of silk suddenly shot from its spinnerets—thumping into Toby's back.

'What the heck is wrong with you?' he screamed at the spider. It was as if it had a personal grudge against him.

The spinnerets rapidly clicked together, reeling him towards his doom. Toby struggled, but only succeeded in dragging the spider closer to the edge of the cola pool. If it got out, that would make matters worse for him.

He looked around for anything he could use—and spotted a paperclip. He dived towards the clip and scooped it up—just as he was tugged closer to the spider.

With a grunt of exertion, Toby pulled a section of the bent paperclip straight. He only needed to extend one spar to form a spear; the rest of the clip provided the perfect grip. He charged the spider.

The evil looking eyes saw him coming and the beast tried to incept him with its clicking fangs. Toby charged the arachnid with all the momentum he could muster. The paperclip speared through the creature's head— Toby discharging his lightning blast through the metal as it did. The spider's head exploded—splashing green and grey gloop over Toby. His momentum flipped the creature onto its back and pitched it off the edge of the desk.

Toby watched the brute fall—before realizing the silk strand was still attached. He grabbed the silk and fired his lightning blast through it—melting the silk seconds before it could pull taut and drag him down.

Toby caught his breath. He'd only fought two spiders and still had several trillion nanites and a supervillain to face. It was going to be a long day.

He hovered over the edge of the desk to see if he could spot the twins.

'Guys?' he yelled.

He was alarmed to see Sable had entered the room and was snuffling about on the floor. The dog headed straight for the two spider carcasses and licked them up, before snuffling around on the floor where Toby had left the twins.

'NO!' he screamed. He had the dreadful thought that the mutt had eaten its owner. As much as he disliked the twins, he didn't want that to happen to them. He would have to break from the plan and enlarge himself to save the twins.

He selected the power from his phone and instantly felt his body swell. It was one of the most unpleasant experiences he had ever had and he felt thoroughly nauseous afterwards. He fought not to be sick, the last thing he wanted to do was lay a sea of puke over the twins—no matter how tempting that sounded.

Sable was alarmed to see Toby suddenly appear in front of him, but barked and danced around him, licking the spider gunk off him—which had also grown proportionately.

'Sable! No! Bad dog!' Toby grabbed the dog by the collar and pulled him out of the room, slamming the door behind him. He walked carefully over the carpet, just in case he trampled the twins.

'Guys?'

He saw a patch of black on the carpet where they had barbecued the first spider. Toby carefully knelt down and peered closer.

'Can you guys hear me? OW!' Something pricked his cheeks. He turned in time to see another miniature fireball arc out from the gap under a set of drawers. The twins were there, waving to him. He could see their mouths move, but could hear nothing. He had expected them to have comically high-pitched voices like in the cartoons, but real life wasn't always funny like that. He held out his hands for them to climb on.

'You're alive!' he whooped.

The twins dropped to their knees, covering their ears in pain. Toby suddenly realized that his voice must sound like a rock concert. He dropped to a whisper, which helped.

'I'm glad you're OK,' and he surprised himself because he meant it. 'The nanites are here. I think it's best if I take you with me.'

They nodded in agreement. He dropped them into his breast shirt pocket, and made a mental note not to shove anything in there later. He just hoped they didn't grow back to normal size anytime soon.

He turned to leave the room—just as all the windows imploded!

Jagged glass and splintered sections of window frame spun towards him. He dropped to his knees as multiple glass shards stabbed into his back. It was painful, but his healing power fought against any serious injury—without that, he would have been shredded alive. He checked the twins were safe before flying through the broken window.

There was a battle raging below. Two of the Downloaders lay prone on the floor, possibly dead. Toby looked around for their attacker—before realizing the remaining three Downloaders were ganging up on Jen!

Furious, he dropped to Jen's side and faced the attackers. Lightning flared from his fingers threateningly.

'Back off!' he warned the rookie Downloaders. They looked at him with puzzled expressions—something was wrong. 'Jen? What's happening?'

He turned to look at Jen properly. The nanites had

synthesized her! The side of her face was crawling with tiny nano-bugs. The nanites crawled all over her skin as they grafted her mobile into her skull, using the technology as a receiver to control her. She looked at Toby with undisguised loathing—then shot at him point blank!

0
1
0
1
0
0
0
0
1
1
0
0
1
0
1
0
1
1
0
0
1
0
0
1
0
1

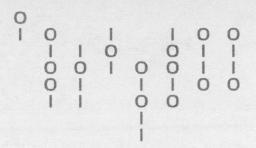

A Small World

Flames covered Toby's field of vision and he could smell his hair burning. The jet of fire burnt his skin without mercy. The force of the strike lifted him off his feet and threw him a dozen metres into a stagnant pond.

He splashed down in the stale water, which, mercifully, quenched the flames. He lay there, allowing the water to cool him down. His skin made horrible sickening sounds as it healed—the fireball must have ripped the flesh away to his bone. Once more he was thankful for downloading the extra-healing ability. His mission hadn't even properly started yet and it had already saved his life a couple of times.

He combed his fingers through his hair—or what was left of it. It had burnt away to a rough crew cut. The healing powers didn't fix cool haircuts, so he would have to look like a marine for the next few months.

He suddenly remembered the twins were in his pocket and sat upright, checking they were OK. They had been submerged for the last half minute and spluttered and swore at Toby. Luckily he couldn't hear a word they said.

Jen was now a major problem. How could he stop her without badly injuring or killing her?

He checked his phone was working; luckily it was waterproof and fully functional. He looked up to see one of the remaining three Downloaders plucked off her feet and tossed onto a rooftop. She tried to stand, but was swallowed by the Swarm. He watched in horror as the nanites disassembled her. She was still screaming as the machines plucked off her skin and worked their way through to the muscles and bone beneath. In seconds she had been deconstructed, each element of her body being used elsewhere within the Swarm for fuel or replicating other machines. It was a terrible sight to witness and Toby felt physically ill. He knew this was something that was going to haunt his dreams.

He had to act fast and without mercy. He remembered an expression: *the needs of the many outweigh the needs of the few*. No matter how much he cared for his friend, the fate of mankind was at stake.

As quickly as he could, Toby soared low over the ground and reached the two downed heroes as nanites swarmed towards them. He didn't have time to check if they were still alive—he needed their phones and the valuable powers they carried.

A Small World

The last surviving guy—who could have been Tony—leapt over to Toby's side.

'What're you doing?'

He was suddenly blasted off his feet before Toby could reply. Fortunately his phone dropped at Toby's feet. He scooped it up—ducking just as Jen's energy blast shot overhead.

'Come and get me!' he roared at Jen.

Toby shot vertically up and Jen followed. It was the only way he could think of buying time.

He flew through the Swarm, the tiny machines felt like hailstones as he cut a path through them. He finally emerged on the other side, high above the Swarm and fog.

Some nanites still clung to his skin and clothes. The tiny machines crawled up on him. Toby channelled a lightning shock through his body, instantly electrifying himself. The tiny machines shorted out, falling away.

He only had seconds to activate one of the Foundation phones he had swiped—just as Jen punctured through clouds beneath him. She snarled and hurled a stream of fire at him.

Toby banked away—then dropped, performing a tight spiral that brought him slightly below her. She tried to compensate for the sudden move, but it gave Toby enough time to activate the power he required on the phone—

A miniaturization cone shot from the device and consumed Jen. He heard her scream as he administered the full charge. An after-image of Jen lingered as she shrank to a microscopically small particle—far smaller than Toby and the twins had been rendered.

He could no longer see her—but at least she was neutralized for the moment. Toby quickly changed direction back towards the Swarm, knowing she had no chance of following him now she was so small.

The fate of the world lay on his shoulders—again. But this time he was on his own. That was a sickening prospect.

He hovered above the swirling cloud and carefully extracted the extra raw power phials the Foundation techs had added to his phone. They contained a powerful electro-magnetic pulse power that would, theoretically, instantly wipe out the nanites. The only problem was the blast would not be powerful enough to take out the entire Swarm that encompassed half the world. However, he had faith in Emily's wild plan. He just hoped he had the opportunity to execute it.

He hovered and pulled the rifle from over his shoulder. He loaded the EMP, Electromagnetic Pulse, cartridges into the gun. He had six shots. Six shots to save the world, leaving one left on his phone.

'Here goes nothing,' he mumbled to himself and dived into the roving Swarm beneath him.

A Small World

Again, the nanites slapped into him like hailstones. Toby adjusted his trajectory so he was no longer plummeting earthwards, but instead heading deeper into the Swarm. This was only the edge of a nanite mass that stretched to both sides of the Atlantic, but at least he was inside the Swarm. He reckoned that he had seconds before the Swarm reacted to the foreign infiltrators and rended him apart. All he had to do was shrink down to their size—smaller than before. He had to push the power to the max.

Toby activated his phone, and gritted his teeth as his body was suddenly jolted. His stomach lurched worse than before—it felt as if he was falling into infinity.

For a second, Toby's vision went black—then suddenly flicked through all the colours of the spectrum in rapid succession. When his sight came back he thought he had been transported to a strange parallel world.

The entire sky, in every direction, was filled with planets. It took him several moments to register that he was looking at the nanites from a vastly different perspective. Some had been the size of a fly; others had been no bigger than a grain of sand, but now they were incredibly massive.

Toby landed on the surface of one that was, proportionately, the size of an aircraft carrier. The smooth surface was warm to the touch. The tiny circuitry channels he had seen earlier were as large as roads. Energy pulses shot through in pairs with loud whooshes.

Above him, the Swarm kept in perfect formation. There was no sense of movement. The outside world was now so vast, and so far away, he could see nothing but a grey blur.

Regular laser pulses shot between the nanites; it was like beautiful multicoloured lightning. He remembered reading in the Project Swift files, about the nano-laser optics that sent signals between the individual bots to trade information.

The machine he was currently hitching a ride on sported massive drilling appendages that stretched as tall as tower blocks. The front of the nanite slowly rotated like a drill as it cut through the air. This was the same type of machine he had seen on the window earlier; the same type of bot that would have disintegrated the Downloader to dust. For his plan to work, he needed to reach one of the communication drones.

A smaller machine hove into view. This was about the size of a small frigate and covered in hair appendages. Massive sail-like paddles pushed the machine through the air like a whale through the ocean. A series of tubes along the machine's central hull shot the laser information beams to the other machines. Toby recalled from the files that this was a communicator, which was exactly what he needed.

Toby took flight and crossed to the communicator. He landed on the side without any fuss. This looked as if it was going to be easier than he'd ever dared hope.

As he landed, he realized that the machine was huge relative to his own size. It was constructed from dozens of over-lapping panels, bonded together with a hard glue substance. Toby had to get to the central processor unit inside. The CPU was a state-of-the-art optic processor that ran the machine and dictated its role within the Swarm, and the only way in lay through one of the many laser tubes.

As Toby approached, the lasers fired out their regular signal. This close, he could feel the wall of heat from the lasers that were as thin to him as a pencil. Luckily the laser tubes were wide enough for him to fit inside. At the bottom he could see the laser lens, a large unblinking red eye. If he got caught in the tube when the laser fired, he would be vaporized—and no amount of super-healing would save him. He had to time it right. Drop in, and then smash through the tube into the nanite's interior hull.

He waited patiently for the lasers to pulse again. The madness of the situation gripped him. In reality the communication nanite was 0.005 millimetres in size—no larger than a small grain of sand. Yet here he was, standing on it as it glided through the air in a coordinated display with trillions of its mechanical cousins.

The information lasers shot out in all directions. As soon as the column of light vanished, Toby flew into the tube. It was stifling hot inside and he knew he should be sweating, but was a little concerned he wasn't. Perhaps his pores were too small for the sweat to seep through?

He hovered over the lens and punched the side of the tube. The metal buckled, but remained intact. He tried again with similar results.

'Come on! Give me a break!' he yelled.

Several more punches dented the metal, but it didn't give. It was like pounding pliable plastic.

The lens below him suddenly whined to life—it was powering up again. Toby frantically kicked at the tube sides to no avail. The lens started to glow blood red—in seconds a laser pulse would be shot out again.

In desperation Toby shot his lightning bolt. The sparks that leapt from his fingers were thick and cumbersome—but they did the job. A small neat hole was punctured through the tube. Toby struggled through—as the laser flared behind him, the heat wave singeing his skin. It was a narrow escape.

He looked around the cavernous interior. He had

been expecting it to be laid out like the decks of a ship, but instead he was surprised to see that it was hollow; an arrangement of girders that kept the hull rigid. At the centre of the machine was the giant CPU.

'There you are!' exclaimed Toby. He pulled his gun, loaded with the precious EMP cartridges, off his shoulder and flew across to the CPU—within minutes, he'd know if their wild plan would work.

Midway to the processor, something collided with him sidelong, spinning him into a girder. The object that had hit him hovered menacingly. It was the size and shape of a football, sporting nasty spikes in every direction. A pair of nasty prongs, mounted on the side, crackled with power. It was a security bot, originally designed to break down cancerous tissues. The machine had been reprogrammed by NanoMite to seek out any undesirables—like Toby.

A fine laser shot out and burnt Toby's leg. He howled in pain, dropping from the girder. Lightning arced from his fingers and blew the irritating machine in half.

Toby smiled . . . then saw two dozen more machines that had been hanging from the walls suddenly detach and head straight for him.

'Aw, hell . . . ' was all he managed before they opened fire simultaneously.

The explosion ripped a massive hole in the side of the communication bot, blowing off one of its large paddling fins. Toby tumbled out, a horde of security machines in pursuit.

He spun out of control before crashing into the side of another aircraft carrier sized nanite. He watched as the communication centre he was about to sabotage spun out of control and collided with three more machines with an explosive result as its laser discharged.

As soon as that happened, a rapid series of signals flashed between every other hulking machine he could see—the alarm had been raised. The machines knew they had an infiltrator.

The smaller security drones buzzed towards him as the massive machines around him edged closer in response to the intruder. Toby wasn't sure what was happening—until the hundred massive nanites around him fired a fine mist from vents in their sides.

They'd sprayed a cloud of security bots: thousands of them, all zeroing in on Toby!

Toby raced along the curved deck of the nanite he had landed on. Gravity didn't normally work in this ultra-small world. Each of the mighty nanites created its own micro-gravity through strong atomic forces, known in the scientific community as 'strong force'.

There were few places to hide on the wide-open hull. Several hundred guns fired at the same time—the results were catastrophic.

The onslaught tore the nano-cruiser he stood on in

half. The hull severed in a smooth tear that glowed from the extreme heat.

Luckily, Toby was clinging to a section the size of several football pitches. It rotated, providing cover from another hail of lasers that blasted a huge chunk from the wreckage. Everything floated as though they were in zero-g, which created a cloud of debris that shielded Toby from the security bots. There was no way he could survive a direct hit from a thousand of them.

The drones fired short controlled bursts at the floating debris, breaking it into smaller chunks. Another series of nanites swept into view, about the size of garbage trucks—these had yawning mouths that scooped up the junk. They were processing craft that would break down the junk into component parts and recycle them throughout the Swarm.

But Toby didn't have time to marvel at the efficiency of Professor Epstein's creation—because they were about to kill him.

He had one option left. He raised his rifle towards the security drones and fired from the hip as he'd seen soldiers do in the movies.

The EMP pulse discharged from the rifle, shimmering the air. Toby kept the trigger depressed until the first ampoule of power was empty. The effect was extraordinary. The thousand-strong horde of security drones suddenly hung limply in the air while dozens of the bigger nanite 'cruisers' behind, that lay in the firing line, suddenly deactivated and spiralled lazily through the air drifting out of formation. Several crashed into one another—but there were no explosions, just the crunch of hollow shells bouncing apart.

The unaffected nanites outside the EMP's blast suddenly peeled away as they tried to vacate the battle area.

Toby whooped victoriously. Several thousand down—just a few trillion more to go! The principles of the plan worked—he now just had to apply it to the Swarm.

His sixth-sense made him turn round—a fast-moving object was heading in his direction.

Toby kicked away from the hulk he was standing on and hovered in the air, rifle aimed for whatever the Swarm could throw at him next. He looked through the optical gunsight and saw that the approaching menace was Jen; Toby almost dropped the weapon in surprise.

Jen came to a halt, hovering opposite him. Toby could see her skin was crawling with nanites, some no bigger than ants—they had obviously shrunk when Jen had.

'You cannot defeat the Swarm, Toby Wilkinson.' The sound came from Jen's mouth, but it wasn't her voice, it was NanoMite's.

A Small World

'I wouldn't count on it,' Toby replied coolly. 'If you really thought there was no threat then you would have made Jen attack me instantly.'

Jen remained silent. Toby guessed the EMP pulse had sent a flurry of warning messages through the Swarm, which had allowed Jen, or the possessed Jen, he corrected himself, to locate him.

'I compute that you are no threat,' said NanoMite. 'Or else you would have struck now rather than play for time. This will be your undoing.'

Jen fired a jet of liquid fire towards him. It was easily dodged. There was something odd about the flames. They seemed too big to be effective. The microscopic size was having a strange affect on some of the powers.

'Now that was rather pathetic,' Toby goaded. 'Do you want to try again?'

Jen roared in fury and tracked Toby's movements as he orbited around her. Her eyes glowed bright yellow and a string of pulsing spheres shot out. Toby ducked to one side—but the spheres homed onto him. This one wouldn't be so easy to avoid.

Toby glided to the nearest nano-craft. This one had plenty of towers and gullies he could lose himself in—it was like flying through downtown New York.

The energy spheres banked and weaved in his wake. He took one corner at the last minute—two orbs crashed into the side of the structure in an explosion of blinding light. He lost another three in a similar manoeuvre—but two more remained close on his tail, slowly catching him up.

He swerved towards Jen, accelerating to ramming speed. She had no intention of getting out of his way. At the very last second, Toby came to a complete stop and changed direction at a perfect right angle. Ordinarily such a manoeuvre would have seen his guts ripped apart from the change in g-force, but at a macro level he felt nothing.

The chasing spheres slammed into Jen before she could move out of their path. Toby felt bad as he watched her spin out of control towards another massive craft. Her skin was red raw from the explosion. She had downloaded the same healing factor as he had done, so he wondered why her wounds wouldn't heal. Instead, the nanites would keep her alive as long as possible, but if he hit her again it would kill her.

Jen landed awkwardly on the hull of another huge nano-craft. Toby bore down on her.

'Jen? Speak to me!'

This close, he could see one side of Jen's face was covered in silver nanites. The remaining half was still flesh and blood but a huge section of that now hung off in a grotesque lump. He could see the muscle and bone beneath. He wanted to be sick. Nanites flooded into the wound, bonding it together and turning her into more of a machine.

'Jen?'

WHAM! She punched him with such force, Toby was surprised his head didn't fall off. He must have fallen unconscious for a second because when he opened his eyes, he was flat on his back and Jen was standing over him with her fist raised. Nanites trickled along her arm, forming a lethal spike on the end of her fist. She punched down with sledgehammer force.

Toby had just enough presence of mind to roll sideways as the spike punctured the deck below. Before Jen could retract the weapon, Toby hooked his legs around her arm and tensed them—effectively trapping her arm in place.

'I'm sorry,' he said.

If there was anything left of his friend, it didn't register on her face. In a quick movement, Toby fired his rifle into her chest.

The invisible EMP pulse shot through Jen's body. She staggered backwards—then keeled over. Toby scrambled to her side.

'Jen? Speak to me. Please . . . don't die!'

He cradled her head. As he moved her, the chunks of junk that were implanted into her face fell away as the nanites bonding them together deactivated.

Then the chunks of wiring that were embedded in

her skull started to push themselves out of her body with a sickening crunch. Toby watched with a combination of repulsion and amazement. Her super-healing must have been dampened by the nanites to enable them to graft to her skin. Now they were gone, the healing factor was pushing all foreign objects from her body.

Jen suddenly gasped, her body jerking as metallic objects clattered out of her. It sounded like a lot of loose change falling. The wounds quickly healed as her abilities fought to save her life. It was a magical transformation; in just over a minute she was back to normal. Her eyes flicked open and she gazed at Toby with blurry eyes.

'Where am I?'

Toby beamed with relief. He wanted to kiss her . . . but didn't. 'We're inside the Swarm. They had synthed you. You tried to kill me.'

'Huh?' She gasped in pain when she sat upright. 'I must be losing my touch if you're still alive.'

'I thought I'd killed you.'

She flashed him a cheeky smile. 'There's no chance of that, shrimp. No matter how zoned out I am.' She stood up, her strength flowing back. 'So, where do we kick butt?'

Toby felt a rush of relief now that he was no longer alone in his task. He pointed to one of many communication nanites that had moved out of the way of the

A Small World

EMP pulses. 'We go in there. But we only have four charges left. I don't know if that'll be enough to knock out the entire Swarm.'

'It's going to have to be. Shall we?'

They soared towards the nearest communicator. Toby had warned her about the security drones inside. They only had one shot to burst in and offload their payload.

Now he knew the hulls were empty, Toby didn't waste any time with the laser tubes. He smashed straight through the hull and into the hollow interior.

Jen followed, and in a wave of devastating plasma blasts, she destroyed the security drones before they could peel away from the wall.

Toby flew straight to the optical CPU. He activated his phone and called up the one power that would allow them to complete their mission—it would atomize him, sending him into the CPU exactly the same way NanoMite travelled.

'Are you sure you know what you're doing?'

'Certain. I digitize in with the EMP powers. Trace the origin of the Swarm back to wherever NanoMite is storing Pete's stolen replication powers—combine them with the EMP cartridges and we should have a self-replicating EMP pulse that will travel throughout the Swarm, destroying it.'

'You make is sound so easy.'

He smiled as he checked the optical processor. It was then he saw the flaw in his plan and his smile vanished.

'What's the matter?'

'There's no way in to the processor! Look.' He thumped a solid block of metal that protected the CPU. The only way in was through narrow vents that he couldn't even put his finger through. 'I did this when I escaped from the Council of Evil. Then I had a monitor to jump into. Here there's nothing! I need to touch the processor but it's protected by the damn case!'

He had carefully read the Foundation instructions regarding this power. If he couldn't touch the electronics then he would simply turn into a bunch of charged particles that would be dispersed into the air.

'We could tear it off?'

'Tear the cover off, that would shut the CPU down and it would disconnect from the network meaning I'll be trapped inside.'

'So we need to go smaller.'

'Impossible. We've used all that power. There's nothing left.'

He felt the crushing certainty of defeat weigh heavy on him. They had come so close.

'What about them?'

Toby frowned. Jen was pointing at his chest. He looked down to see Jurgen and Hayden hanging over the lip of his pocket, waving for attention. They had heard every word.

Toby held out his hand and let them climb out. He was stunned to see them. He had simply assumed that once he'd shrunk they would have been left behind; instead they had miniaturized in proportion. He had no idea you could double-shrink people. He carefully laid them next to the CPU. Hayden squeezed into the intake vent and out again indicating they could fit.

'Do you guys know what you have to do?'

He saw Hayden gesticulate and rapidly speak . . . but they could still hear nothing.

'We can't hear you. Just nod or something.'

The twins gave two thumbs up. Toby was sure he could see a resigned look on their tiny faces, and it occurred to him that this could be their last mission. He tried to think of something poignant to say, but couldn't think of anything.

Toby laid the last three EMP cartridges next to the twins—they were three times their size. Despite this, the twins' enhanced strength was still working and Jurgen heaved one over each shoulder. Hayden grabbed the last then held up his mobile phone to show Toby it was still working. Toby had downloaded the digitize power to everybody's phones just in case it was their last means of escape. It was now proving to be their only means of defeating NanoMite's Swarm.

Toby wanted to warn them not to mess this mission up, but bit his tongue. They were showing incredible bravery. Despite their natural clumsiness, their hearts were in the right place.

They were real heroes, and for once, he felt proud for having been the one who had trained them up. He hoped this really wasn't a one-way mission.

The twins disappeared through the narrow cooling slots on the CPU case, dragging the EMP vials with them. Two flashes from within the system indicated they had successfully digitized themselves and were now running along the cyber pathways of the Swarm.

If they knew this was a suicide mission, they were making sure they completed it to the letter.

Jen and Toby looked at one another. Hanging around in the centre of the storm was not a safe place to be. Besides, the moment the twins deactivated the Swarm, they had to move in to confront NanoMite.

That's when they would face the real battle.

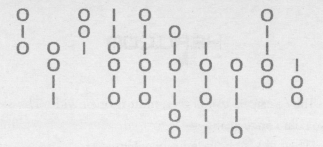

Chain Reaction

Toby and Jen teleported out of the Swarm, aiming a good distance away from the encroaching cloud of death. It had almost spread to Germany's northern edge and was heading towards Denmark where the Government could do nothing but evacuate their people further north.

Minutes dragged painfully by as they waited for any sign that the twins had been successful. After ten minutes, both Jen and Toby snapped back to full size. The subsequent nausea did nothing to brighten their mood.

Toby leant over a wall, dry heaving—until Jen nudged his arm.

'Look!'

The nanite Swarm had been growing on the horizon, a black stain against the blue sky. It suddenly flickered with internal lightning and a deep sustained boom washed across the landscape thirty seconds later.

The cloud flashed with increasing intensity—then it was suddenly swept away as if a hurricane force had blown it apart.

Toby jumped to his feet, mouth open wide. The sky was blue once again.

'They did it!' he cried jubilantly.

Jen screamed with excitement and hugged him tightly. They performed an improvised victory dance.

Toby was the first to sober up. 'I hope they're all right.'

Jen suddenly calmed as if she'd been tranquillized. 'Yeah . . . I'm sure they are.' She sounded uncertain.

Toby took a deep breath. 'Our turn now.'

The undulating hills around the river Rhône were beautiful, stretching to the north and east into gentle alpine peaks. Or rather, the landscape would have been idyllic if it hadn't been covered in an ashen grey cloud of nanites and metallic dust that smothered the life beneath.

Jen and Toby quantum tunnelled into a field in the small town of Flévieu, across the river from the *Superphénix* nuclear facility that NanoMite was using as a base. The quantum tunnel was a stealthy way of travelling that allowed them to sneak up on their enemy. Unlike teleporting, they could make multiple jumps in quick succession—ideal for the commando raid they were embarking upon.

Chain Reaction

Their first reaction was that they had made a dreadful mistake—the nanites were still here.

Then a ripple shot through the grey dust at supersonic speed—evaporating the nanites beneath their feet. Toby breathed a sigh of relief; they had merely outrun the path of self-replicating destruction the twins had set in motion.

Across the river, the dust fell from the huge cylindrical tower at the heart of the abandoned power station.

Toby was suddenly brimming with confidence. 'Let's do this.'

NanoMite convulsed with anger. His feet stomped against the floor as he threw a tantrum. He had sensed the sudden EMP detonations within the Swarm. They had radiated out from the location he had stored Pete's replication power. He had swarms of nanites using the power to replicate themselves into an unstoppable army—then some stupid heroes had thrown in a raw electromagnetic pulse power. Pete's superpower had instantly combined with the EMP energy and replicated in an unstoppable chain reaction that had wiped out his Swarm.

In five minutes his entire network had been evaporated! With half the world under his control it had seemed like an impossible task—but now power had been restored to cities; world militaries had regained control of their weapons and the Hero Foundation had suddenly put Hero.com back online. His master plan was unravelling.

The EMP wave was so quick that he had been forced to disconnect himself from the Swarm before the pulse was transferred into him. Now he was filled with vitriolic rage.

The people he had kidnapped to form his neural computer system physically felt the destruction of the nanites. They convulsed as if the blows were hitting them. The nanites flowing through them suddenly deactivated and the neural-processors all slumped to the floor, unconscious.

To add insult to injury, Professor Epstein's mocking laughter rang in his head. The remnants of the personality were still very much alive.

The air at the end of the chamber suddenly tore apart like a curtain as the quantum tunnel opened. NanoMite could see the idyllic valley outside.

'What is this?' he bellowed.

A blast of frost suddenly shot out, engulfing his body in a solid block of ice.

Toby and Jen flew into the chamber and quickly took stock of their new environment. It was fifty metres in diameter, and they were positioned halfway up the tower. Luckily, Toby had read the schematics beforehand to ensure they didn't tunnel into the main reactor that lay below them. The reactor core dominated the centre of the room, with access platforms circling the core's exterior. Above them lay a massive corroded yellow crane system that ran on rails and was used to raise and lower the cooling rods into the reactor when it was functional.

The kidnapped victims lay on a platform near the wall, safely out of the way. Toby hoped they were all alive. He recognized Yvonne from the sea of faces, the trip to whose apartment had led them here. It looked as if she was peacefully slumbering.

The ice around NanoMite suddenly cracked as the nanites that formed him super-heated.

'You have already tried that,' NanoMite's voice was filled with contempt. 'It won't work twice.'

'It's game over for you,' retorted Toby. 'Can you thank Professor Epstein for his help in bringing you down?'

NanoMite roared in frustration and extended both hands, firing a pulse of white-hot energy. Toby and Jen darted in separate directions as it struck the floor where they had been standing, forming a crater. Toby suddenly doubted the wisdom of having a shoot-out in a nuclear reactor, even a decommissioned one.

He perched on the lip of a reinforcement girder that ran along the perimeter of the tower.

'You just don't have the skills to defeat us, Nano-Mite. We've faced worse than you.'

'You mean "better than you", surely?' shouted Jen from across the reactor. 'If they were worse, then they wouldn't be as good as this clown.'

Toby nodded graciously. 'I believe you're right.'

NanoMite looked between the two heroes with disgust. 'This is not the time for a lesson in grammar!'

He blasted Jen with an intense energy volley. The wall and floor bubbled from the impact—but there was no sign of Jen.

Her laughter drifted from the crane overhead, where she clung on the girders like a monkey.

'You've got to be faster than that,' she taunted.

Although they were both flicking light-hearted banter at NanoMite, they didn't feel jovial. They knew their one advantage lay in upsetting the villain's delicate emotional balance so he wouldn't suspect their plan. They had to wear him out in order to get close and finish him off.

'We're always one step ahead,' Toby added.

'Enough of this!' NanoMite spat. 'You may be one step ahead, but a grand strategist always thinks several steps ahead of their opponent.'

Toby saw the sudden movement. NanoMite's six

Cohorts stepped from the shadows. Their hands glowed menacingly. Toby recognized their faces from the missing people reports Kirby had showed him.

'They're just kids.'

'Correction. They are highly trained, bionically enhanced kids.'

The Cohort suddenly sprang forward with huge bounds. They bounced from wall to reactor to stairwell to reach their targets. Toby had never seen anything move like them—their implanted nanites gave them extraordinary speed and strength, but their moves showed the split-second timing of seasoned Parkour free runners that Toby had seen racing through the city, leaping over anything in their way.

In seconds, two kids had joined Toby on the narrow girder. They landed either side of him and delivered swift karate chops with their glowing hands. Toby took flight as they sliced into the wall.

However, a third kid was waiting for him. It was Trevor—using his skills honed over hours of game play, he had developed cutting-edge techniques and timing that had made him stand out as one of the best gamers in the world. Like his companions, his physical body was no match for the rigorous activities they played in the games, but with the nanites enhancing their bodies, they were unbeatable.

Trevor soared through the air after calculating Toby's

trajectory in the blink of an eye. He landed on the hero—the extra weight plummeted Toby to the ground.

The two kids perched on the girder somersaulted off the edge to join in the fight below. Their enhanced frames allowed them to land in a stylish crouch around Toby. Their fists absorbed the impact and cracked the concrete floor.

From ten metres above, Jen was convinced she was safe from the ninja kids, as they clearly couldn't fly. But they didn't need to. They bounced from girder to support strut in an amazing gymnastic display to reach her. They surrounded her on the crane, high above Toby.

Toby's first thought was that he couldn't risk hurting them, as they were not responsible for their actions. That was rapidly replaced with desperate thoughts of survival as the Cohorts rained down an ultra-fast array of spin kicks and martial art punches—every move learnt from a computer game and practised until they had blisters on their thumbs. They now played out their moves for real, thanks to nano-technology.

The fight looked like a speeded up video. No sooner had Toby's head been kicked backwards than another Cohort had punched him in his vulnerable extended stomach forcing him to convulse forward. It was a merciless onslaught and Toby could hear his bones breaking—then rapidly healing. If he didn't do something then it would be an endless cycle of pummelling until his powers expired and he was beaten to death.

Jen dropped off the girder to avoid her attackers. She had seen what had happened to Toby when he had flown, so she zigzagged to avoid being plucked from the air.

It didn't work.

One of the kids missed her and crumpled against the central reactor core. He spun to the ground like a mannequin, his arms splayed at awkward angles until the nanites knitted him back together. Two of the Cohorts grabbed her in midair. The weight of one was enough to pull her down—but two fat kids made her drop like a stone.

Concrete cracked as she hit the ground with ferocious force. The Cohorts pinned her down, punching her with lightning fast blows.

Toby was starting to tire. What he gained in superpowers was of no advantage against the Cohort's augmented speed.

'Flash dance!' he exclaimed through bloody lips.

NanoMite was watching his victory with a sense of glee. His Swarm had been defeated, but his Cohort had saved him from complete failure. He had assumed Toby's last utterance was to do with the brain damage he must surely be suffering. Only at the last moment did he see the earpiece Toby was wearing glowing blue.

Ordinarily his nanites would have neutralized any electronic device, but the only ones he had left were keeping him alive or controlling the Cohort.

To everybody in the room, Toby appeared to vanish.

Toby felt the superpower rush through his body. Then the world suddenly ground to a slow motion ballet as his perception speeded up. The Cohort still moved fast but, to him, they now appeared to be moving at normal speed.

He ducked two synchronized punches and kicked the third kid in the knees. It was an inelegant assault, but with his super-strength it broke both his attacker's kneecaps. He dropped to the floor allowing Toby to bolt towards Jen.

She now had all three of her Cohorts trading punches as she tried ineffectively to crawl away from them. Toby barrelled into them like a bowling ball. They had not expected the attack and spun away in every direction.

However, no matter how fast he was moving, the Cohort was still quick. His original three assailants were already charging towards him. Toby didn't have time for niceties. He raised his hands and blasted the rusting steel girders holding the crane up. His super-fast shots sawed through the metal almost instantly and the heavy crane dropped.

He watched impatiently as the crane descended with

all the urgency of a feather. Toby surged up to intercept it. He gripped the edge and, with a combination of super-strength and speed, he hurled it towards the ground to speed its descent.

The thirty-ton crane flattened four of the Cohort. A quick energy blast sent the remaining two reeling into the curved walls.

NanoMite couldn't keep up with the action. He watched helplessly as his Cohorts were bashed around by a fast moving blur—then the crane fell at an alarming speed—pinning more down.

A grinning Toby suddenly appeared in front of him. He waved his phone at the villain.

'Game over, NanoMite.'

Toby thrust his hand into NanoMite's chest—

But NanoMite's body quickly formed a hole as the nanites avoided Toby's punch. Toby quickly retracted his hand and the nanites closed the hole.

NanoMite's laugh was not pleasant. 'You fool! Haven't you learnt yet? My nanites know all your moves and tricks! You can't pull the same trick on me twice!'

Toby glanced behind him as the Cohorts stood, pushing the heavy crane off them. The micro-machines had rapidly healed them. Jen moved closer to Toby, covering his back. She was still feeling groggy from the beating she had taken.

NanoMite continued taunting him. 'It is you who is defeated!'

'Now, Jen!' shouted Toby.

'Huh?'

'NOW!'

Jen suddenly remembered what she had to do. She slid out her mobile and dialled Toby's number.

NanoMite stalked towards them. 'I will make your deaths . . . ' he suddenly trailed off when a funky ringtone echoed through the reactor. He looked around trying to trace the source. Then he looked at Toby.

Toby smiled, elated that their wildly optimistic plan had worked. He held up his empty hand—the hand that *had* been clutching his phone.

NanoMite suddenly clawed at his stomach—that's where the ringtone was coming from! Toby had dropped the mobile inside him!

'You may have been thinking a dozen steps ahead . . . but I was always thinking about the winning move,' gloated Toby.

For a moment, NanoMite's expression flickered to a smile and he clearly heard Epstein's voice: 'Thank you!'

Then the EMP pulse stored in the phone exploded inside NanoMite. Toby and Jen held each other as they ducked—millions of nanites exploding in every direction. The electromagnetic pulse radiated across the reactor—destroying the last of the nanites.

Chain Reaction

The Cohort suddenly slumped to the ground as the machines inside them were destroyed.

It was over in seconds.

Toby and Jen slowly stood up, not quite believing they had won despite overwhelming odds. Jen looked at him with an admiring smile.

'You know, shrimp, you have the making of a hero after all.'

The next day was a whirl of activity, but all Toby had wanted to do was sleep. The kidnapped victims that had formed NanoMite's neural network had been dropped off at ordinary hospitals, and they were all making speedy recoveries with no memory of the ordeal they had been through.

The Cohort kids had to be tended in a Foundation hospital to surgically remove the tech implanted alongside their muscles. The same applied to tens of thousands of people all around the world who the nanites had synthed.

Toby had been in touch with his parents, who had assumed he'd been isolated, like them, because of the massive power outages. They seemed fine, although Toby was still deeply worried because he had heard nothing back from Lorna.

Around the world, Governments provided excuses

for the mysterious fog clouds and power shortages, anything to avoid mentioning the existence of superpowers. It would take a few months for cities to clean up their respective messes, but at least the loss of life had been kept to a minimum.

The high point had been when Jurgen and Hayden had shown up alive in a field in Germany having fallen to earth with the nanites. They had expanded back to their normal size once the power had worn off. They took great delight in wooing everybody within the Foundation HQ with their incredible story of battling through the Swarm's virtual network and delivering the EMP that stopped NanoMite's stranglehold on the world.

Toby listened in silence for a change. His usual feelings of jealousy were replaced with pride that his cadets had performed superbly when it really counted. This time he agreed that they really were heroes.

But the twins were not about to ignore their friends. Toby was surprised when they hoisted him and Jen onto their shoulders and told everybody who the real geniuses were behind the plan. The crowd went ecstatic when the full story emerged.

Jurgen punched Toby's arm. 'Toby, congratulations! I never doubted!'

'Jurg . . . you called me "Toby"!'

Jurgen frowned. 'Is that not correct?'

Chain Reaction

Toby and Jen burst into laughter. Tears streamed down their faces leaving Jurgen even more confused.

The day ended with a minute's reflective silence when Eric Kirby's death was formally announced. The head and creator of the Hero Foundation would no longer be steering the mighty heroic organization, and with Chameleon still missing, nobody knew who would.

Toby watched the weeping staff with a sense of detachment. The previous day, as Kirby was dying, the control room had been the scene of a stupid party. Now it was a scene of mourning.

Toby found himself alone in Eric Kirby's office, and it was there he finally cried. No matter what he had done, Kirby had believed he was doing the right thing. Toby couldn't blame him for anything. He had left some riddles—why had he stalled attacking the Council of Evil when Toby had finally discovered its location? And who exactly were the Inner Circle and why were they so influential?

He suddenly noticed something hanging on the wall, held in a glass frame. It was a folded shirt with a faded 'CC' logo: Kirby's old Commander Courage uniform. It was still smeared with dirt and dried blood from when Toby and Pete had saved him in the jungle during World War Two. That was, chronologically, the first time Kirby had met the boys—but it was far from the first time they had met him. He had never noticed that

Kirby had kept them as a precious reminder of that moment.

That thought stopped Toby's tears from rolling. The sadness he had been feeling was suddenly replaced by an odd sense of completion.

Kirby owed them his life, but if it hadn't been for Kirby then he would never have been a hero, and who knows, maybe the world would never have been saved. It was all a series of random events, which had, bizarrely, made sense.

Toby stared at the shirt and wondered what the future held, for him, Jen, Pete, Emily, Lorna and the twins. What strange new adventures would rise from the chaotic events of the present?

Only time would tell.

Andy Briggs was born in Liverpool, England. Having endured many careers, ranging from pizza delivery and running his own multimedia company to teaching IT and film-making (though not all at the same time), he eventually remembered the constant encouragement he had received at an early age about his writing. That led him to launch himself on a poor, unsuspecting Hollywood. In between having fun writing movie scripts, Andy now has far too much fun writing novels.

He lives in a secret lair somewhere in the south-east of England—attempting to work despite his three crazy cats. His claims about possessing superpowers may be somewhat exaggerated . . .

Chaos Effect is his fourth novel in the fiendishly clever 'Hero.com' series, and follows *Council of Evil*, *Dark Hunter*, *Power Surge*, and *Collision Course* in the deviously dark 'Villain.net' anti-series.